# KING DAVID

## FAVORED, FALLIBLE, FORGIVEN
## *(JUST LIKE US)*

ARTHUR D. BRIGHT

# TABLE OF CONTENTS

# AREA MAP

(M-1)

# INTRODUCTION

King David is a heroic figure that has captured the minds and hearts of generations for thousands of years. The many facets of David includes his battle exploits, his leadership qualities, his love for God, and his love for Israel's people. He is also known as a bad boy making his myriad of characteristics the reason why so many of us can identify with David.

Dr. Gene A. Geltz, in the book series *Men of Character*, wrote about King David. He titled the book's Introduction, "A Man Just Like Us."[1] His book inspired me to read more about King David. What I've read motivated me to share my findings and thoughts about this very popular and much loved man. I've always heard King David referred to as "God's beloved" or "a man after God's own heart". I wondered, how can we measure up to a person with such a reputation? But then, as I read more about David, he appeared less mystical, he seemed more human, and like us, vulnerable to temptation.

Getting to know more about David's life helps to understand how he would still be called God's beloved in spite of his sinful behavior. Recognizing David is no better or worse than we are helps us to realize, in spite of our own behavior, we too are still God's beloved!

An often asked question, "How can we compare our lives to those in the Old Testament; it's so long ago and things were so different?" We are able to compare our life experiences, to their lives, because our histories are linked to the same God.

The book strives to show how God's relationship with His children, during King David's life, mirrors our relationship with Him today. Essentially, this book illustrates how believers in those times fought temptation and endeavored to be obedient. Today we reflect the same struggle with temptation, and like them exert efforts to be compliant. The book also makes a concerted effort to highlight the privilege God has given us to have a personal relationship with Him. David's life is a vivid model of the consistent effort required to establish an intimate relationship with God. It also illustrates the struggles we will encounter holding on to that relationship.

King David often had difficult periods in his life when he had to make multiple and tough decisions. There were many moments when he lacked the knowledge to make the best or even a good decision. But during those arduous periods he deliberately took the time to spend quiet moments with God. It was during one of these times he came to realize that God's lessons are taught during difficult times. He also comprehended the key to reaping the benefits from God's lessons, is to hold on to Him tight while in that storm.

It has been over three millennial from David's time to now, and God is the Constant throughout this whole period. Times and circumstances have changed but God has not; so like David, we must nurture God's timeless Spirit within us. God loved the believers of the past, as He graciously does us today. Neither God nor His Word will change. Kenneth Chafin states in his publication *Mastering the Old Testament": 1, 2 Samuel*, The story of David and Bathsheba dramatizes David's *humanness* in an unforgettable way. It also reminds us when accomplishing His purpose *God always is forced to use fallible people.*"[2] People *Just Like Us*!

# CHAPTER 1

# THE CLAMOR FOR A KING

*"THE SPIRIT OF THE LORD HAD DEPARTED FROM SAUL"*

*(1 SAMUEL 16:14A KJV)*

We open with Israel's Elders traveling to Ramah to demand their spiritual leader and judge, Samuel, inform God they want a king. They desire to have a monarchy like other nations. One reason is they feel Samuel is becoming less effective at executing his duties. But the real concern is the fear of Samuel's wayward sons coming into power. Samuel apprehensively tells God of the people's request; he knows his Lord will feel rejected by His people. Truthfully, Samuel is the one who feels unwanted; he is irritated by their ungratefulness. He doesn't relish the idea of relinquishing his power and prestige, at the prime age of 55, to a rookie king. Not only will a monarchy diminish Samuel's role as the judge of the people but it will also eliminate his role as Israel's military leader. And as the Elders' feared, more important to him is his life-long desire for his sons to take over his roles and respective duties when he dies.  To Samuel's dismay, God consents to the people's request.  God describes the person Samuel is to choose as king.

This is the beginning of a new era in Israel's history.  The people are overwhelmingly pleased with the selection of Saul of Gibeah to be their King.  Saul is 30 years-old, from a prominent family, tall, and handsome.  Samuel was also pleased with the selection; he personally knows Saul's father, Kish, a devout man and member of the tribe of Benjamin.  Samuel doesn't think much of Saul; he has already experienced two unimpressive observations of him.  The first being when Saul was confused trying to find his father's stray donkeys.  The other is when Saul was hiding behind the baggage cart at the moment Samuel is announcing him as the first King of Israel.  Samuel deduces he can still retain his status after witnessing Saul's immature behavior.

During the first two years of Saul's reign he is restless and decides he will lead his army to engage in some minor skirmishes, most of which are easily won.  But Saul's two years of procrastination allows the Philistines time to strengthen their forces.  Finally, when the Israelites face the Philistines' 36,000 man army, the Israelites are petrified.  At the sight of the huge military force, they scatter in different directions, some hiding in caves, while others seclude themselves on the hillside.

Hearing of this embarrassment, Samuel instructs Saul, "Wait seven days before entering into another battle for I will return and administer a sacrifice to God, asking for a victory." But Saul ignores Samuel's instructions and decides to take matters into his own hands.  Saul performs a sacrifice, well knowing it is forbidden, for he is neither a prophet nor priest.  As soon as Saul finishes the ceremony, Samuel happens to show up.  *"And Samuel said to Saul,*

*Thou hast done foolishly: thou hast not kept the commandment of the LORD thy God, which he commanded thee."* (1 Samuel 13:13 KJV) Saul's poor choices reinforce Samuel's confidence that he can maintain control over the new monarchy.

Territorial wars are constant and they serve the purpose of gaining prestige and power, as well as reaping the vast monetary rewards attained when conquering nations. For several years the new King Saul has had success at winning mostly minor battles. It is now time for Saul to move up to the big leagues. Samuel instructs him, *"Now therefore, heed the voice of the words of the LORD."* (1 Samuel 15:1 NKJV) God instructs Saul to take on a war of revenge against the Amalekites. God remembers the Amalekites' mistreatment of the Nation of Israel during their exodus from Egypt 500 years ago. One of God's specific instructions forbids Saul taking any valuables; the Amalekites and their belongings are to be completely wiped off the earth. Personal greed overcomes King Saul and his men. They disregard Gods command and take treasures. Saul also spares the life of Agag, King of the Amalekites. Then brazenly he sets up a monument to himself in Carmel. Upon arriving, Samuel questions Saul about his pride and obvious disobedience. Saul fakes religious enthusiasm and gratitude; he lies and proudly proclaims, "The spoils have been taken for a sacrifice to the Lord." But he cannot answer Samuel's question, "Why is Agag still alive".

It is quite obvious to Samuel that Saul has replaced the Spirit of the Lord with the darkness of his flesh. He prays all night asking God to give Saul one more chance. God denies the request and takes His Blessings from Saul's kingship. God also instructs Samuel to demonstrate His displeasure for Saul's acts of disobedience, *"And Samuel hacks Agag in pieces before the LORD in Gilgal."* (1 Samuel 15:33 NKJV)

# CHAPTER 2

# DAVID, "THE STOCK OF JESSE!"

*"AND THERE SHALL COME FORTH A SHOOT OUT OF THE STOCK OF JESSE, AND A BRANCH OUT OF HIS ROOTS SHALL BEAR FRUIT."*

*(ISAIAH 11:1 ASV)*

King Saul has reigned for 21 years when we meet David, who is nine. David has the hated job of managing the sheep; fundamentally herding, grazing, and protecting them. He performs these duties with his four dogs who are his only companions. David's daily routine consists of caring for his sheep and his dogs while studying and meditating on God. David intentionally prioritizes his daily devotion to God as he manages his routine duties of managing the sheep. When David is herding the sheep he is worshiping and praying, and when the sheep are grazing he is studying about Jehovah or playing his instruments to keep the sheep calm. He is always watchful for God's voice and at all times listens intently to what God has to say. David cherishes the times he spends with the Lord. The Cornerstone for his and Israel's future is being constructed during these years.

David lacks a personal relationship with his father, Jesse, a well-known man in Bethlehem. Jesse is looked upon as an honest business man, as well as a pious man whom God has blessed with seven sons, and two daughters. David is the youngest son and frequently clashes with his six brothers who are much older. David's family only acknowledge him as the "sheep boy" and never see anything more. Unfortunately for them, they don't appreciate his strong faith, and fail to recognize David's intimate relationship with God.

David's gifts are incomprehensible, and his brothers are envious of him. Their blindness doesn't allow them to associate David's competence as being God's favor. They do not equate these attributes to the Spirit in him. By not spending much time with David they are unaware of the amount of devoted time David spends with God. They are unaware of the man that David is becoming.

But David doesn't fault them for not understanding; he often wonders himself how he is able to achieve what seems impossible. Early in life he supposes it is God; next he acknowledges it is God; as he matures he accepts his achievements could not have been accomplished without God. David is bewildered that God continually blesses him and shows him such grace. At this early stage of his life, David has no clue of God's purpose for him.

*"Jesse begot Eliab his firstborn, Abinadab the second, Shimea the third, Nethanel the fourth, Raddai the fifth, Ozem the sixth, and* **David the seventh***. Now their sisters were Zeruiah and Abigail. And the sons of* **Zeruiah were Abishai, Joab, and Asahel**—*three."* (1 Chronicles 2:13-16 NKJV) David's life of solitude changes when one of his sisters, Zeruiah, moves back home after her husband dies. Grandpa Jesse insists they return home. "Without their father,

Zeruiah cannot properly raise those three wild boys, Abishai, Joab, and Asahel. There needs to be some men in those boys' lives."

Jesse has vast landholdings; he comes from the stock of Obed, and is the grandson of Boaz and Ruth, prominent landowners themselves. Jesse has several houses situated on an abundance of land that can comfortably accommodate them all. The three nephews are older than David yet in age they are closer to David than David is to his brothers. The nephews are assigned to work for David managing the sheep. Even though they are older David is told to instruct and supervise them. Zeruiah's sons may be older in age, but Jesse knows they are not as mature; David can survive in the wilderness alone, they can't.

Early on in this sprouting relationship, the nephews become keenly aware of the wisdom uncle David has at his young age. They eventually realize it's because of his close relationship with Elohim. Asahel, the youngest of the nephews, has a strong belief in God, more so than both his brothers. Asahel is immediately attracted to David because of his obvious special relationship with God. This close relationship with David gives Asahel the good fortune to be around when David writes his Psalms. At their young age, Asahel and David accept as true that God uses people to speak and act for Him. They believe some people are put on mission to help His children continue on their ordained path.

Joab, the second to oldest nephew, is drawn to David for different reasons. He admires David's evident leadership skills, his fighting ability, and David's gift for influencing others. Early in their relationship Joab also recognizes the politician in David; in time he becomes David's closest collaborator. Abishai, the oldest nephew, is the boisterous type; he is a ready and able fighter, but more the intellectual type in a secular way. His attraction to David is the comfort he has in David being in charge; he recognizes David is a strategist, and a warrior. Abishai shares David's love for the Israelites, and he respects God and admires David's devotion to Him.

The four boys have been together on a daily basis for three years. During this period most of their time was spent herding, and shearing the sheep, and oftentimes chasing predators. Occasionally they would get an opportunity to venture into Jesse's vast and thickly wooded landholdings. There they learned how to survive the rigors of the wilderness, including how to hunt and fish. Over these years they have become very close friends. The nephews are the first to realize that God has chosen David for *a special purpose*. They've witnessed God protecting David many times. After three years the four boys are anxious to find out, what is David's *special purpose?*

# CHAPTER 3

# THE SECRET ANOINTING

*"I WILL SEND THEE TO JESSE THE BETHLEHEMITE:*
*FOR I HAVE PROVIDED ME A KING AMONG HIS SONS."*
*(1 SAMUEL 16:1B KJV)*

When God takes His blessings from Saul, He already has a substitute King in place. God calls on Samuel at his house in Ramah. He orders him to visit Judah and anoint a son of Jesse the Bethlehemite, as His choice for King. Samuel voices concern, "My Lord, I fear King Saul will kill me if he finds out You have commanded me to anoint Jesse's son to be King." God reminds Samuel, as Circuit Judge and Priest he customarily makes sacrifices and judgments in different localities, so this visit should cause no alarm. God assures Samuel the passing of the crown is not eminent and the public's awareness of it will not be soon.

Jesse's receives a notice Samuel will be visiting his home. For Jesse, Judge Samuel personally visiting him and his family is very disturbing; why the visit? He is nervous. On the day of the scheduled visit all are outside anxiously waiting for Samuel to arrive. That is, all except David, who was not asked to attend. Asahel declines the invitation and stays with David and the sheep. Joab and Abishai are present with the family, but stay in the background. Nathan arrives, and after a period of introductions, Samuel informs Jesse of his reason for being there: to anoint one of his sons to be the next King. Jesse is relieved the visit is not negative. But at the same time he is shocked, along with being extremely proud, that God chose to anoint one of his sons the next King of Israel!

God is about to teach a lesson to His people, including Samuel the Prophet. God has had His eye on David forever; He's been grooming David for this specific role and mission. God demonstrates how His planning exceeds man's thoughts, and how His ways are more profound. God allows all to see Jesse's oldest sons get rejected as candidates for the anointing. God doesn't want the tall or worldly experienced brothers. God lets reality sink in for a moment, *If not them who could it be?* At this same moment no one is even considering David as the likely candidate. God prompts Samuel to ask, "Is there another son?" Jesse pauses and remembers David, "Yes, my youngest son who manages the sheep" (minimizing his significance). Immediately Jesse orders Joab to fetch David.

God often will lift-up those who have been overlooked and stepped on the most; in this family, David is the bottom rung of the ladder. God has long been preparing David to be the King of Israel, even before his birth. If there is going to be a King, God wants that person to be someone who knows Him, hears His voice, and ultimately brings His children closer to Him. By the time the Elders' had gained enough courage to make their request for a King, God had long ago implemented His Plan for David to be King.

As David is walking, he looks ahead and sees all his family

members who astonishingly seem to be waiting for him.  He immediately takes notice of this special-looking man he does not recognize.  What impresses David about Samuel is the deference he
sees his father giving him; something he never seen his father doing for anyone else.  After God affirms to Samuel, *"this is the son"*;
Samuel informs David, "God sent me to anoint you the next King
of Israel;" causing family members' jaws to drop.  Samuel anoints
David's head with oil symbolizing he is God's choice to be Israel's
next King.  For David this is a significant benchmark in his life-long
relationship with Jehovah.  At twelve years old, David's faith is now
increased even more.

David's nephews are not surprised at all about Saul losing the
throne; many people had suspicions about Saul's devotion to God.
For some people, the power and prosperity that emanates from
receiving God's favor tends to make them drift away from God;
this has become the people's opinion of Saul.  On this Spiritual
journey David and the nephews will learn, frequently our human
side will try to hijack God's Plan and put our own strategies into
play.  And even after God's repeated rejections of our plans, and
the subsequent failures of the same, we often still don't get it.  To
succeed, our plan must be congruent to the plan He has for us.

Back at the palace, Saul's behavior has his personal servants
worried and scared.  Since God dumped him, he has been acting
distraught, and displaying erratic behavior.  Saul's servants suggest
a remedy for the King's anxiety; they want to send for a young
minstrel who plays a soothing harp, and lives not far from the palace.  *"And Saul said unto his servants, Provide me now a man that
can play well, and bring him to me." (1 Samuel 16:17 KJV)* God is
working His Plan.  The servant recommends contacting Jesse of
Bethlehem, who is a loyalist and is known to be prudent; Jesse has
a son who is a capable musician.  When notified, Jesse is reluctant

to send David but has no choice. Jesse packs some gifts for David to give to the King demonstrating his loyalty, humbleness, and respect for authority. Jesse never misses an opportunity to stay in favor with power. David throws his harp over his shoulder and proceeds to the palace. After being there only a month, all are pleased with David's musical talent, and its positive effect on the King. The King's stress is relieved, and consequently there's less anxiety in the Kingdom. David is placed on the royal payroll.

# CHAPTER 4

# THE ANOINTED GIANT SLAYER

*"NOW THE PHILISTINES GATHERED THEIR ARMIES TOGETHER TO BATTLE, AND WERE GATHERED TOGETHER AT SOCHOH, WHICH BELONGS TO JUDAH; THEY ENCAMPED BETWEEN SOCHOH AND AZEKAH, IN EPHES DAMMIM."*

*1 SAMUEL 17:1 (NKJV)*

Since the time Saul disobeyed God during his fight against the Amalekites, he has remained on God and Samuel's "bad list". Samuel is doing his best to hold the nation together until God publically declares there is a new King. Three years have gone by since David was anointed and during these years he's been regularly playing the harp for King Saul.

It's at this time Israel's' army has come together at Sochoh in Judah to defend against the invasion of an historical enemy, the Philistines. Jesse's oldest boys, Eliab the firstborn, next to him Abinadab, and his third oldest son Shammah, went off to fight in the war. David and his nephews have been taking food to his brothers since the war began for in these times it is customary for the citizens to provide provisions for their army. The confrontation has continued for over a month when Jesse tells David to take more supplies to his brothers. Joab notices Jesse's special gift of cheese to the Captain helping him to further discern the root of David's learned political skills. Jesse knows how to work the system; it's in his genes.

David finds his brothers in the midst of mass hysteria and confusion. Goliath, a giant Philistine, shows up twice a day excoriating Israel's army, and rebuking Israel's God. The Israelites are petrified of Goliath. When the nephews finally decipher Goliath's ranting they immediately look at David to see his reaction; they know David, and as expected, David is furious. David turns to his nephews screaming, "Who is this heathen cursing the God of Israel. And, why are God's people doing nothing about it?" In David's emotional state Abishai has to help him realize "God's people" are in fear. He reminds him, "You must keep in mind, when most others are terrified, you are imbued with God's inner peace." Joab is pumped, ready to fight alongside David.

Historically David and his brothers have stayed at odds with each other. And now their baby brother, with his loud talk, disrespects them in front of their comrades. Still brooding over their loss of God's anointing, Eliab erupts, "You just came to the war front to belittle and embarrass us again. There is nothing you are capable of doing about the situation, return home and mind the sheep". David hears the men snickering, but he is undeterred, his center of attention is not on his brothers. David is totally focused on defending God's honor. *"And David spake to the men that stood by him, saying, What shall be done to the man that killeth this Philistine, and taketh away the reproach from Israel?" (1 Samuel*

*17:26 KJV)* The fear of Goliath has the 57 year-old Saul mystified and paralyzed with fear; confirming the Spirit of the Lord has truly abandoned him.  In panic Saul has offered rewards, including his daughter Mereb, to anyone who will accept Goliath's challenge; with no takers to date.

David gets an audience with the King; he immediately lets the King know he is not seeking a reward.  "My purpose for volunteering is to kill the blaspheming Philistine, and defend God's honor." While David is making his request to fight the giant Philistine, Asahel and Joab are close by waiting and listening.  The King is amused at the young David who shows no fear.  Saul and his entourage discount David, only thinking of him as the young man who has been playing the harp these past three years.  But David's nephews are very aware of who David is, and who he is defending. They know God favors David, and they believe there is no fear in David, only faith.  Both have often witnessed God intervene on David's behalf.  As a result, they trust David will slay the Philistine. On the other hand, with the expectation of a fatalist, Saul half-heartedly gives David permission to fight Goliath.

This is one of the examples where we can see reflections of ourselves in the Bible.  We can compare how God fights believers' battles, then and now.  Most often the battles are bigger than we are.  Goliath is bigger than David but David received gifts years ago that prepared him for *"such a time as this"*.  David grew up protecting the sheep from all predators including bears, wolves, lions, and thieves.  Years of experience protecting the sheep allowed David to acquire unique traits: he has great instincts; he's agile, cunning, and physically fit.  All these attributes are wrapped up in his unshakable faith in Jehovah.  David confronts the giant Philistine, *"And the Philistine said to David, Come to me, and I will give thy flesh unto the fowls of the air, and to the beasts of the field." (1 Samuel 17:44 KJV)*

In Buruch Halperns' book, *David's Secret Demons* he expresses his thoughts on David and Goliath's well-known contest.[3] His commentary made me envision a focused David mentally drawing a circle around Goliath and his shield bearer.  If the two got close to the edge of the circle David would quickly maneuver to another location.  As per custom the giant is weighted down with considerably more than 100 pounds of armor plus his spear.  And as David anticipated, Goliath gets worn out chasing him.  Now David has a slow moving target for his slingshot; he takes the shot.  David's smooth stone hits the target, knocks the giant out, and as he's falling to the ground, his armor bearer drops the shield and runs.  David seizes Goliath's sword and cuts off his head.

Killing the blaspheming Philistine makes David a hero.  Of course after the giant is slain his nephews have their chests poked out, and for sure, David's relationship with his three brothers is estranged even more.  Naturally, there are doubters and haters, including Saul who becomes jealous over the praise being given to David.  Before Saul presents his oldest daughter Mereb to David, as publicly promised, he adds a provision: David must conquer more of Israel's enemies, *"Only be valiant for me, and fight the LORD'S battles." (1 Samuel 18:17a NKJV)*

Asahel believes that God is using King Saul to advance His Plan for David, which obviously does not favor Saul.  Asahel tells his brothers, "Saul must not yet know that David has been anointed to be the next King of Israel.  He is unwittingly giving David the keys to the throne by providing David with a leadership role in an army of thousands.  This gives David a platform to further demonstrate he is a leader and capable of protecting Jehovah's people." Asahel is adamant in his belief that God uses whomever He desires to further His purpose; for example: King Saul today and His use of Pharaoh Centuries ago.

Joab is delighted; finally the lessons learned will be utilized, and like David, he will become recognized as a leader and a warrior. Abishai suggests to his brothers to be cautious about trusting Saul who only wants the spotlight on himself, which David's shadow tends to block. Abishai is on point, Saul did have a hidden agenda: *"For Saul thought, "Let my hand not be against him, but let the hand of the Philistines be against him." (1 Samuel 18:17b NKJV)*

# CHAPTER 5

# JONATHAN-FAMILY-NOB

*"AND DAVID SAID UNTO AHIMELECH, AND IS THERE NOT HERE UNDER THINE HAND SPEAR OR SWORD?"*
*1 SAMUEL 21:8 (KJV)*

At 15, David becomes the 42 year-old, Prince Jonathan's Armor Bearer. Jonathan admires David for his authenticity as well as being a courageous young warrior. After several battles they befriend one another; a bond is formed. They eventually make a covenant, and Jonathan honors David with a gift of his robe and sword. Spending years with his father and David, Jonathan is astute enough to see they have conflicting personalities that puts them on a collision course. Overtime Jonathan will become trapped between his love for his father and his friendship with David.

In character, Saul continues his conniving ways and marries his daughter Mareb to someone else. He offers David a consolation prize, his daughter Michal, but with a third round of conditions.

Always scheming Saul takes advantage of the fact David comes from a family that does not have the appropriate wealth or power commensurate for marrying a King's daughter. Saul appends a surcharge on his second marriage proposal: David must bring the King 100 foreskins of the Philistines. David ignores the King's lack of appreciation, and disregard that he has already; *"taketh away the reproach from Israel"*. He displays no ill will towards the King, but demonstrates to him Who is controlling matters. David brings the King 200 foreskins and Michal becomes his wife. The nephews are glad for David. It is evident David is on an ordained path, and they are excited and determined to be on the route, with and for him. Abishai reminds them that King Saul will be unyielding holding onto his throne, not excluding killing David if need be. The brothers vow to be as relentless guarding his back.

*"Now the distressing spirit from the LORD came upon Saul as he sat in his house with his spear in his hand. (1 Samuel 19:9a NKJV)* Saul tries to kill David with his spear for the second time. David flees the palace. Saul's paranoia is escalating because of David's rising popularity with the people. Jonathan tries to remind his father of the good things David has done for the King and for Israel to no avail. Saul cannot comprehend how his own son can take David's side. He wonders, *doesn't Jonathan realize that David is a threat to him as heir to the throne?* Saul sends his messengers to David's house and if Michal had not helped David escape through a window he would have been taken prisoner and executed.

Saul had mistakenly believed it would be to his advantage if his daughter was David's wife. It is becoming evident that God is using everyone, friend or foe, his children included, as instruments to move David closer to fulfilling His plan. Aware of the outcomes of these incidents, Asahel is convinced God will continue to guide and protect David, and will not permit any third party to interfere with David's mission.

After being a member of the King's court for seven years David is now a 22 year-old fugitive on the run. He goes to his spiritual mentor, Samuel, and lives with him at the school in Naioth. Saul finds out that David is in Naioth and after sending several emissaries there, who do not return, he goes there himself. Upon arrival he sees his men prophesying and immediately Saul goes into a hypnotic state and he starts prophesying, enabling David to escape again. *"Then David fled from Naioth in Ramah, and went and said to Jonathan, "What have I done? What is my iniquity, and what is my sin before your father, that he seeks my life?" (1 Samuel 20:1 NKJV)* Jonathon assures David that his father will not kill him. Jonathan loves both David and his father, making it an agonizing situation for him. Putting himself in jeopardy, Jonathan continues to defend David. For instance, the king expects his entire family to be at the Feast of The New Moon. David being his son-in-law, the delusional Saul expects David to be there even after trying to kill him. So, when David does not show up on the second day of the Feast Jonathan again is forced into the position of defending David. Saul orders Jonathan, "Go find him, and bring him here so I can kill him!" *And Jonathan answered Saul his father, and said to him, "Why should he be killed? What has he done?" Then Saul cast a spear at him to kill him, by which Jonathan knew that it was determined by his father to kill David. (1 Samuel 20:32-33 NKJV)*

Jonathon hastily leaves the Feast to meet David and tell him he must disappear, his father has bad intentions towards him. They make a covenant, *'May the LORD be between you and me, and between your descendants and my descendants, forever.' "So he arose and departed, and Jonathan went into the city." (1 Samuel 20:42 NKJV)* David leaves quickly to escape the King and to avoid causing Jonathan more trouble. Jonathan didn't mention his father tried to kill his own son!

David heads to Nob in Benjamin near Jerusalem on the Mount of Olives; a city of priests in the line of Eli. Ahimelech, the head priest, guardedly approaches David for he has never seen David without his army; he has only a few men with him. David tells him he is on a secret mission for the King. David asks for food and weapons. Ahimelech hesitantly gives him and his men showbread to eat; it's a violation of the Law of Moses; only the priests are supposed to eat showbread. After eating, Ahimelech gives David the same sword that he used to kill Goliath. God continues to provide. While these interactions with Ahimelech are occurring, David notices Doeg, the Edomite, who is Saul's Chief of the Herdsmen, spying on their transactions; he surmises Doeg will surely tell King Saul.

The King's pursuit of the renegade David continues throughout Judah's wilderness. David ends up in a cave in Adullam, on the borders of the Philistia plain at the base of the Judea Mountains. David's family learns of him being in Adullam and they immediately seek him and happily find him there. David's parents, Jesse and Nitzevet, his brothers, and their neighbors, are constantly being harassed, and persecuted, by Saul's army. Saul believes they are hiding David. *"And everyone who was in distress, everyone who was in debt, and everyone who was discontented gathered to him. So he became captain over them. And there were about four hundred men with him." (1 Samuel 22:2 NKJV)*

This is the first time Jesse has seen his baby boy since David fled from King Saul. Jesse reflects on the shock and honor of God's anointing of David; his gallant slaying of Goliath, and his son being a victorious leader in the King's army. Though these events make Jesse a proud father, he is taken aback by the fact he was not mindful God was grooming his child. But as a pious man Jesse does not question God's ways; he is thankful for, and humbled by His ways. He reaches out and gives his boy a long hug. The weight of Jesse knowing how neglectful he was to David as a child is lightened because of the unfathomable favor God has shown them, for he and David are closer now than ever.

This is a joyful moment, a turning point in David's ordained journey. Abishai cheerfully comments, "It took David's family all these years to realize he is God's chosen one. Notice the joy in David today, his family is finally proud of him and showing it." Asahel reminds everyone, "See how God continues to cultivate David. God is showing David, on a personal basis, the needs of His people, *So he became captain over them*." God is revealing to David the reason why his life is being protected and channeled in a specific direction."

The commentary, *Bible History Old Testament* says, "To the king of Moab, whose protection he could invoke in virtue of their descent from Ruth the Moabite, he commended his father and mother."[(4)] The Moabites are one of the people Saul attacked unsuccessfully when he first became King. David knows Saul will not go there; there is no love for Saul in Moab. But there is plenty of love in Moab for Jesse's clan; Ruth is a notable Moabite, and Jesse is Ruth's grandson. David leaves Adullam for Mizpeh of Moab; he plans to leave his parents there in the country of his ancestors to be safe. What a homecoming this is for Jesse.

Meanwhile, Saul is in Gibeah raging at his men and frantic that he is being conspired against, even by his own family. He asks for those who are loyal to step forward and help him find that traitor, David. The Edomite, Doeg, reveals what transpired with David and Ahimelech at Nob. The King sends orders for Ahimelech and the entire priesthood to come to him for questioning. The King is furious at the priests for aiding David with food and a weapon; he also accuses them of plotting against him. After questioning, and dissatisfied with the answers, Saul orders his personal guards to kill all 85 of the priests; they refuse. Doeg is glad to ingratiate himself to the King and volunteers for the assignment; he kills all the priests demonstrating his loyalty. And when they arrive at Nob, Saul is angry that David got away. He orders Doeg to kill every man, woman, and child, along with their animals, for their disloyalty to him. Saul is providing a vivid illustration of what will happen if anyone supports and/or conceals David.

This massacre fulfills God's prophecy that the bloodline of Eli will go extinct, and so it did except for one. Abiathar, Ahimelech's son, is the only survivor of Nob. He escapes and finds David. Hearing what happened in Nob, David is distraught, he blames himself, *"So David said to Abiathar, "I knew that day, when Doeg the Edomite was there, that he would surely tell Saul. I have caused the death of all the persons of your father's house." (1 Samuel 22:22 NKJV)* David assures Abiathar that he can remain with him and he will be safe. Asahel tries to console David assuring him that he couldn't have known this would happen. Abishai wonders if God used David as a means to fulfill His prophesy that the line of Eli would become extinct. Joab, true to character, feels David should have taken Goliath's sword and killed Doeg when he first noticed him snooping. On what the nephews collectively agree is this mistake undoubtedly is etched in David's mind. It is an unforgettable lesson: don't leave loose ends.

## CHAPTER 6

# KEEP WALKING THROUGH THE VALLEY

*"WHEN TOLD THAT THE PHILISTINES WERE ATTACKING KEILAH, DAVID REFLEXIVELY ENQUIRED OF THE LORD, SAYING, SHALL I GO AND SMITE THESE PHILISTINES? AND THE LORD SAID UNTO DAVID, GO, AND SMITE THE PHILISTINES, AND SAVE KEILAH."*

*1 SAMUEL 23:2 (KJV)*

David gets word that the Philistines are attacking Keilah, and they are in desperate need of help. His men express their reluctance to fight the Philistines. Many similar, controversial situations have cultivated David's awareness of who he must turn to first for answers. David reaches out to the Lord and is told he will surely defeat the Philistines. His men are still unwilling to get involved. To them engaging in a battle, while Saul is persistently pursuing them, seems too much to take on; more than they can handle. They haven't been with

David long enough to believe if God tells David he will win, it's a done deal!

*"Then David enquired of the LORD yet again. And the LORD answered him and said, Arise, go down to Keilah; for I will deliver the Philistines into thine hand." (1 Samuel 23:4 KJV)* The men acquiesce. Asahel notes, "The reason God has given David a rag tag, inexperienced army, compared to King Saul's highly skilled combatants, is to give David the opportunity to hone his leadership skills. Equally as important, it is a chance for David's men to get a glimpse of his teacher." David has learned to believe in God and he wants his army to learn. He wants them to realize, with God on their side they can conquer even Saul's highly trained army.

Joab is in awe of how David's faith in God has grown over these years. He doesn't share the same passion for God as David or his brothers; but he is respectful and curious; though not a believer. Joab observes how David's relationship with God is becoming more apparent to the men, and how his belief in God is connecting with them. He also recognizes how this linkage impacts the men's confidence in David, resulting in the men enthusiastically fighting with him in battle. Joab, himself is in awe of David's valor. But because his Spiritual immaturity does not allow him to comprehend David's intimate relationship with God, Joab does not understand David's relationship with God is the reason why he is so courageous.

While David and his men are rescuing the people at Keilah, word comes to Saul that David is there. Saul testifies, *"God hath delivered him into mine hand;" (1 Samuel 23:7 KJV)* Unfortunately for Saul, these days God is no longer delivering him favors, which is becoming more difficult for Saul to internalize and accept. David inquires of the Lord asking, "Will the people of Keilah give me up to Saul?" God says yes. After *the massacre at Nob*, God knows the people's fear of Saul will stifle any zeal to support David. Upon

God's advice, David and his now 600 men immediately get out of Keilah. Access to God's counsel is the advantage David has over Saul.

David goes to the mountains in the wilderness of Ziph, two miles southeast of Hebron, and Jonathan meets him there. Jonathan assures David that his father will never find him and he has no doubt David will be King. Jonathan promises to be at his side. Now the people of Ziph are in the same dilemma as the people of Keilah, to who must we show our loyalty? The thought of the "Massacre" also convinces the Ziphites to succumb to Saul's side; they send a message to Saul stating David is in the forest behind their city.

Knowing that Saul's army is close, David and his men continue their defensive movements in the wilderness of Maon. Saul believes he has David trapped in these mountains. As soon as Saul's men have David completely surrounded, *"… there came a messenger unto Saul, saying, Haste thee, and come; for the Philistines have invaded the land." (1 Samuel 23:27 KJV) Again* God steps in and rescues David. His men, knowing they were trapped and witnessing God at work, is causing their feelings of relief to morph into belief. Saul strategically leaves some men behind to be on the watch for David and eventually the scouts report that David is in the Wilderness of En-gedi.

After a quick defeat of the Philistines, Saul returns with his 3,000 men at the summit of En Gedi, near the sheepfolds among the rocky cliffs. It appears he has David trapped again. The Providence of God requires Saul to take a bathroom break. To relieve himself he unknowingly enters into a cave where David and his men are hidden in its recesses. The men's eyes being accustomed to the cavern's darkness see Saul enter, while coming from the brightness outside nothing in the cave is visible to Saul. Saul mistakenly places himself in a very dangerous position. David's men immediately throw down the God card trying to convince David, "It is obviously the Lord's intention for you to kill Saul; God set him up!"

Historians place this cave in the gorge under a water fall. The noise from the water's pounding, would explain why Saul did not hear David creep up on him when he cut a corner off of his robe. Afterward, up high on a hill, and waving the piece of Saul's robe, David tells Saul that he could have killed him. *"Behold, this day thine eyes have seen how that Jehovah had delivered thee to-day into my hand in the cave: and some bade me kill thee; but mine eye spared thee; and I said, I will not put forth my hand against my lord; for he is Jehovah's anointed."* (1 Samuel 24:10 ASV) David asks Saul to let God be the Judge of his innocence or guilt.

Saul responds, *"For if a man find his enemy, will he let him go well away? Wherefore Jehovah reward thee good for that which thou hast done unto me this day."* (1 Samuel 24:19 ASV) That day, a weeping Saul acknowledges his own guilt. He implies David will be the next King. Saul beseeches David, "Swear you will not cut off my descendents;" similar to the pledge David has given Jonathan. Understandably, both the King and the Prince are concerned about their descendants. They fully understand when David becomes King he will have their family's lives in his hands. But Saul's momentary guilt and temporary compassion are not repentance. Saul returns to Gibeah and after a few days he's ranting and raving; he cannot get David off his mind. The King mounts up and begins hunting his rival again. David in contrast goes to God asking for forgiveness for violating Saul, His anointed. He also asked God not to allow him to be influenced by his followers' sentiments. Of course, Joab thought David should have killed Saul when he had the chance.

During these fugitive years Joab is pleased to be learning how strategically to avoid an enemy who may have superior forces, and thrilled just to be a leader of an army. While Joab believes he's on this journey for his own benefit he is actually on mission, serving God's purpose. Though Joab will be recognized for his militarily contributions towards the unification of Israel, he will also be known as the villain in many of his transactions before and after the united Israel is formed. Even though Joab's life script is to protect David's image during the kingdom-building period; he is glad to play his role for now. He's aware his future prominence is dependent today on David's success. But, the long-term ambition for Joab is to be recognized and acknowledged as a major player and a significant reason for David becoming King. Joab's personal aspirations motivate him to unknowingly serve God's purpose.

*"And Samuel died; and all Israel gathered themselves together, and lamented him, and buried him in his house at Ramah. And David arose, and went down to the Wilderness of Paran"* (1 Samuel 25:1 ASV) After David pays his respects to his 90 year-old mentor he and his men head to Carmel. The Wilderness of Paran's area stretches from Sinai to the borders of Palestine in the southern territories of Judea. In this region lives Nabal of Moan who is a prosperous businessman in Carmel. David and his men protected Nabal's herdsmen and livestock from two and four legged predators all winter. It is now spring, a festive period of the year, for it is time to shear the sheep. David feels he should share in the rewards from a successful winter and thus sends a messenger to humbly ask Nabal for supplies. Spontaneously Nabal brusquely rejects the request, and misrepresents David's intentions, saying David's running a protection racket. When David is informed of this affront, Joab notices how David's disposition changes to rage. Without delay David gives orders, *"Gird ye on every man his sword."* (1 Samuel 25:13 ASV)

Fortunately for most, God intervenes through Nabal's servant who speaks to Abigail, Nabal's wife. He tells her, "Master Nabal has insulted David; he has accused David of being an extortionist." The servant counters Nabal's characterization of David's actions; "This past winter, David and his men protected us and the sheep from all types of predators." The fact that the servant can freely speak disparagingly about his master, her husband, demonstrates the contempt everyone has for Nabal. Abigail is an intelligent woman, she knows who David is and his reputation; she also knows how her husband can be a fool. She intercedes, and acting quickly, sends servants ahead with gifts of food and wine to assuage her meeting with David, an indication of her astuteness. On meeting David she humbly voices her heartfelt apologies and sincerely requests forgiveness for her husband's slanderous words. David is impressed with her demeanor and kind words. He can tell she has God in her life. It doesn't get past David that she's beautiful as well; they seem infatuated with each other. Observing their interaction, Joab notices another transformation in David's disposition, a persona he has not seen before.

Abigail tells Nabal what she has done; it seems the shock of his wife's wise and kindhearted behavior causes Nabal to have a heart attack, and he dies ten days later. Some consider his death an act of God, "*And when David heard that Nabal was dead, "Blessed be Jehovah, that hath pleaded the cause of my reproach from the hand of Nabal." (1 Samuel 25:39 ASV)* David is grateful for Nabal's mysterious, convenient death. Abishai asks, "Does David believe Nabal died because he's an insult to God or because he disparaged David." Abishai feels the lines are getting blurred. In spite of his cynicism, Abishai recognizes that God looks out for David in ways no human can. He is pleased that God's path for David is starting to become apparent; the dots are starting to connect. Without responding to Abashai's pointed question about Nabal's death, Asahel agrees David's path is becoming evident, for example, protecting Nabal's sheep last winter produced fruit: *"And David sent and spake concerning Abigail, to take her to him to wife." (1 Samuel 25:39 ASV) "And Abigail hasted, and arose, and rode upon an ass, with five damsels of hers that followed her; and she went after the messengers of David, and became his wife." (1 Samuel 25:42 ASV)* Abigail recognizes the benefit of her marrying the man anointed to be King of Israel and observes David as a person who is close to God.

The positive reception David receives from the town's people is unexpected and happily welcomed. But why wouldn't he receive a great reception? Nabal was hated by the town's people because he treated them harshly. They were happy to see Nabal gone, and he's gone because of David. Asahel blissfully remarks how God had prepared the way for them. "See how the people are exuberant about Abigail and David's marriage." No-nonsense Joab views the marriage to Abigail as not just for love, but additionally for wealth and power; he believes he knows David's agenda. He tells his brothers, "Due to Nabal's death, Abigail is now the richest widow in the area controlled by the Calabites. Strategically the marriage helps David become financially independent and today David is the leader of the Calabites, positioning him to build alliances." To further affirm Joab's theory, David marries Ahinoam of Jesreel, which takes place soon after his marriage to Abigail. David now has two wives, not three, for Saul has given Michel to another man from Gillam.

# CHAPTER 7

# GOD'S INTERVENTIONS

*AND SAUL KNEW DAVID'S VOICE, AND SAID, "IS THIS THY VOICE, MY SON DAVID?"*

*1 SAMUEL 26:17 (KJV)*

The hunt for David continues. The Ziphites notify Saul that he can locate David in the hills of Hachilan; Saul quickly rushes there with his army. David's lookouts see Saul's army coming. They take David to observe Saul's camp where they see Saul with General Abner, the Commander of his Army. David and his men complete their reconnaissance and return to their camp. *"Then answered David and said to Ahimelech the Hittite, and to Abishai the son of Zeruiah, brother to Joab, saying, Who will go down with me to Saul to the camp? And Abishai said, "I will go down with thee." (1 Samuel 26:6 ASV)* Abishai, a courageous warrior, joins David on this ominous mission. Abishai has been with David from the beginning and still is by his side.

Upon returning Abishai shares the adventure with Ahimelech and the other members of the scouting party, "David and I arrived at King Saul's campsite in late evening. With the bright full moon we could see Saul's sleeping area from the mountain top. He was positioned in the middle of the camp with thousands of soldiers surrounding him, and Abner sleeping right beside him. We slowly walked down to the campsite. I admit I was scared but David just kept walking through the rows of sleeping men. He was unwavering, showing no fear. Without doubt it was God's Spirit causing Saul's army to be in such a deep sleep, and I knew it was only because of David; I stuck close by David. As we weaved through the camp we came to where Saul was sleeping; his spear was stuck in the ground beside him. *"Then said Abishai to David, God hath delivered up thine enemy into thy hand this day: now therefore let me smite him."* (1 Samuel 26:8 ASV) At that moment I'm thinking, we can immediately end this fugitive life right now, and David can take his rightful position on the throne, just as God intended. David of course admonished me, *"Jehovah forbid that I should put forth my hand against Jehovah's anointed."* (1 Samuel 26:11 ASV) To prove we were standing next to him, I took Saul's spear and his water jug. We left the camp and, *"stood on top of a hill a great distance between them."* With Abishai holding the King's spear and water jug high in the air, David loudly rebukes Abner for not protecting his King, *"Are you not a man?"*

Saul recognizes David's voice; he attentively listens to David tell him how he could have taken his life again. Saul testifies that he is in the wrong, and David is blameless. God today, is purposely making it obvious to everyone, who is innocent in this feud. David and Saul then go their own separate ways. *"And David said in his heart, I shall now perish one day by the hand of Saul."* (1 Samuel 27:1 ASV)

Back with his brothers, Abishai tells them what happened at Saul's camp, but he speaks more extensively on David's aggravation and weariness from continuously being pursued by Saul. "We all accept we must run because our army is in the hundreds and the King has thousands. But, it is frustrating, and continuous, with no end in sight." Asahel is sure God is allowing these difficult periods preparing David for the myriad of challenges that will come with the crown. David agrees, he is also beginning to believe Jehovah is permitting his troubles, and using the predicaments to foster his growth."

David decides him and his men need a safe haven; a sanctuary where they won't have to be constantly on the run. He envisions a place that helps him keep his army intact, and at the same time allows them to provide for their families. He decides on the land of the Philistines; he's confident Saul will not follow him into enemy territory. The last time David was at Gath, he faked insanity to preserve his life, for he had the reputation of killing many Philistines. Today he has the status of a fugitive, an enemy of King Saul. Moach, the King of Gath, feels it is wise to have David close so he can keep an eye on him, so David is welcomed. David is able to negotiate Ziklag as a location where he and his men can safely reside. David agrees to employ his 600 men as mercenaries and use the rewards to pay the King's son, Achish, a leasing fee for Ziklag.

David's love and passion for his own people prohibit him from raiding villages in Judah. He chooses to covertly get his rent money by attacking Philistine villages located near Judah's borders. To ensure Achish does not discover who David is targeting, David's orders are to kill every man, woman, and child; the brutal order is meticulously executed. Achish is paid Ziklag's leasing fee with his own people's valuables and their lives. The deception works, Achish is more than pleased with the arrangement.

While remaining gallant and loyal warriors, Asahel and Abishai dislike the repeated killings of the women and children. They query amongst themselves if this is God's command or David's personal decision. Jonathan Kirsch, author of *King David (The Real Life of The Man Who Ruled Israel)* says, "The Bible depicts David as a man acting out of *righteous necessity*."[5] Joab agrees; he thinks the population's extermination makes sense and thinks highly of David for being a strong decisive leader. This is where Joab and David's opinions are compatible. Joab knows David can, and will, be ruthless in his efforts to accomplish his mission; he supports David's decision. He suspects it was God who motivated David's moving to the land of the Philistines. He expects God knew David would do whatever was necessary to survive while there. Joab is not alarmed by their present situation of hiding in Philistia; he doesn't believe David's mission ends at Ziklag. Even though David's mission appears to be moving down an unclear path, Joab is confident it's a predestined course.

David pillaging expeditions have been so rewarding, Achish invites David to join his army and engage in combat against Israel. David's perceived loyalty during his 1 ½ years living in the land of the Philistines earned him the honor to be invited. *And David said to Achish, Therefore thou shalt know what thy servant will do. And Achish said to David, Therefore will I make thee keeper of my head forever. (1 Samuel 28:2 ASV)* Achish is offering David the honorable position of being the Prince's personal bodyguard. At this moment it does appear that King Moach has failed to keep, *a close eye on David*.

Our *on-time* God comes to the rescue one more time! He intervenes using Achish's peers as His tools, *"Then said the princes of the Philistines, What do these Hebrews here?" (1 Samuel 29:3 ASV)* David's inclusion in the war effort against Israel is unacceptable; the princes vigorously voice their protest: "David killed Goliath and cut his head off; in order to marry Saul's daughter, he killed 200 Philistines and desecrated their bodies; and, the Israelites still sing hero songs about David's success killing Philistines. We don't trust him." After a back and forth heated discussion with the Barons, Achish, who does not have absolute power, concludes it is prudent not to side with David. Achish tells David he trusts him but the circumstances require David return to Ziklag. The nephews immediately recognize Jehovah has stepped in to get them out of this predicament. Joab chuckles to himself when David says, *"Unto Achish, "But what have I done?"* (1 Samuel 29:8 ASV) Joab admires David's ability to appear sincerely hurt by Achish's decision continuing the charade of loyalty.

Their relief and happiness is not enjoyed for long; the arrival at Ziklag is horrifying. The Amalekites raided their camp and have taken all the women, children, and livestock; the entire village is burned to the ground. David's men blame him for leaving the camp defenseless; they want to kill David. David is in a sticky situation, and as is his habit, he turns to God. With Abiathar's assistance, *"David enquired at the LORD, saying, Shall I pursue after this troop? shall I overtake them?"(1 Samuel 30:8 KJV)* David is seeking the guidance and inner peace God gives to him in these frantic moments. God was affirmative to David's prayer on both counts and even sweetened the news, *"And without fail recover all."* It is a relief and welcome news that their families are still alive. With tears in his eyes, Asahel tells his brothers, "We can thank God for His Grace because the Amalekites did not wipe out our families like we faithfully do to the Philistines."

After days of pursuit they find an Egyptian slave who is abandoned and left to die by the Amalekites. Strengthened with food and water the slave provides the Amalekites' destination. For the purpose of speed David leaves 200 men to watch over their supplies. The remaining 400 ride hard for a day; they catch up to the Ziklag raiders, and defeat them after another day of battle. God promised they would recover all, and they did. Actually, in addition to recovering their loved-ones and belongings, they also took possession of the Amalekites' stolen goods from other raids. David and his men could tell by the clothing the Amalekite's were primarily raiding villages in Judah. On their return to the camp, the four hundred men who vigorously rode and battled for 24 hours are at the point of exhaustion. They feel the 200 men that stayed behind with the supplies should not equally share in the loot; "Getting their families and livestock returned should be reward enough." In response, David without debate immediately establishes a rule that all share equally in the rewards of their battles.

Also, David, *"Sent of the spoil unto the elders of Judah, even to his friends, saying, Behold a present for you of the spoil of the enemies of the LORD;" (1 Samuel 30:26 KJV)* David always keeps in mind how many villagers endangered themselves feeding and hiding his army when they were on the run these past years. Asahel and Abishai now start thinking like Joab; they always understood why David repeatedly performed good deeds, because of the love for his people. But today Asahel and Abishai comprehend it goes deeper than that; David is planting seeds for the future. David gives supplies to those villagers for he plans to be viewed as a King who takes pleasure in sharing with his people. He seeks their never-ending loyalty, and his sharing and caring leadership style, is nurturing their faithfulness. The nephews feel God's decree for David must be close at hand, because the obstacles to prevent David's kingship are escalating.

Achish had drafted David to fight alongside him against Israel. God stepped in and prevented it. At the time when David and his men were rescuing their families from the Amalekites, Saul and his three sons are being slain by Achish and the Philistines at Mount Gilboa in Jezreal Valley. Kings often rode with their armies in battle, and they also were the preferred targets of the enemy. Jonathan and his two brothers, Abinadab and Melchishua, are recognized as royalty. The three are vigorously pursued; they become overwhelmed, and are slain by the Philistine forces. At the battle further south, Saul is struck by arrows, and is mortally wounded. Saul didn't want to be abused by the enemy so he orders his armor bearer to pierce him with his sword. The servant is afraid, reluctant, and refuses, whereupon Saul throws himself on his sword ending his 72 years of life. The Philistines find Saul's body and cut off his head. Saul and his sons' bodies are fastened to a wall to disparage who they are. The people of Jabesh Gilead hear of Saul and his sons' deaths, disrespect, and the denigration of their bodies. Because of a good deed Saul had done for them years ago it emboldens the men in the village to take the great risk of removing Saul and his sons' bodies from the wall, and properly burying them. Remember, this is the battle in which David and his men were temporarily scheduled to participate. God's grace prevented their complicity in Saul and Jonathan's deaths.

Around that same time an Amalekite shows up at Ziklag; he just came from the Jezreal Valley's battle site. He tries to ingratiate himself to David by telling him of King Saul's death. It was obvious by the Amalekite's descriptive telling of what happened he did witness how Saul had died. But he fabricates the tale saying Saul begged him to take his life using the King's sword. The Amalekite again lies and says he reluctantly complied with King Saul's dying wish; he gives David the King's crown and bracelet as proof.

David immediately goes into mourning after hearing of Saul and Jonathan's deaths. Throughout the night, in addition to the continued grieving, a betting pool materializes amongst the men. The bet: when is David going to kill the Amalekite? Outside of David's men, most people did not know the reason David did not kill Saul the two times he had the opportunity; Saul was God's anointed. The next morning David questions the Amalekite again so all can clearly understand he has killed God's anointed. *"And David called one of the young men, and said, Go near, and fall upon him. And he smote him that he died."* *(2 Samuel 1:15 KJV)* Abishai speaks to his brothers, "Listen closely, David is setting rules and parameters for how behavior will be conducted during King David's reign: (1) we are united and equally share the rewards of war along with our people. (2) God's anointed is not to be harmed regardless of his behavior."

Jonathan is the best friend David has had. David grieves for Jonathan. The elegy David shares is commendable for it speaks of the loving relationship Jonathan had with his father, and how the two were unified. These tender words are spoken without even a whisper of the animosity that prevailed over the last 8 years. David wants this speech to be recorded and read to coming generations so Saul and Jonathan will be remembered commendably.

# CHAPTER 8

# A CROWN FOR THE ANOINTED

*"AND IT CAME TO PASS AFTER THIS THAT DAVID INQUIRED OF JEHOVAH, SAYING, SHALL I GO UP INTO ANY OF THE CITIES OF JUDAH? AND JEHOVAH SAID UNTO HIM, GO UP. AND DAVID SAID, WHITHER SHALL I GO UP? AND HE SAID, UNTO HEBRON."*

*2 SAMUEL 2:1 (ASV)*

David spends a private moment of reflection with his nephews, his close confidants. "The past eight years we could have been King Saul's loyal followers if only he had shown a little love. Instead he persistently demonstrated so much hate. As you three have been loyal to me I would have been the same to Saul. But we must not question, but try to understand, God has His own ways and reasons for doing things. The years as fugitives taught us valuable lessons, most importantly, we must depend on God. We shall continue on this journey together, and the four of us will build Israel's new nation." The 30 year-old King David gives his first command to his newly appointed War Counselor, Joab, "Bring my parents from Moab to Hebron."

When David leaves, Asahel tells his brothers how thankful and blessed he feels to have been chosen as a partaker in David's journey. Spiritually filled he speaks, "We were there during David's early days and we quickly became aware of his special relationship with Yahweh. We witnessed how he was looked down upon by his brothers, and overlooked by his father. For God's anointing, you two saw the Prophet Samuel pick David's brothers one by one, and witnessed God reject them all. We observed the whole family's astonishment when God instructed Samuel to anoint David; we have been eye witnesses to God at work.

He continues reminiscing, "We've spent three years in the woods with David caring for sheep. David spends the next three years soothing the King's nerves. Then all of us fight the King's battles for seven years after that. And for the last eight years we've been living in caves and off the land while dodging and hiding from the King. The significant message that evolves out of those 21 years is: *David inquired of Jehovah.* It's become his consistent behavior. David came to the realization a while ago that only with God leading can he fulfill the mission for which he is entrusted. We must grow to that same understanding."

"My two brothers, now after readying him by way of that circuitous and preparatory path, God tells David go to Hebron and become the King...our God is good!" And Hallelujah, it's not over yet; there is still an extensive journey ahead, with many more tough lessons to learn, and much more wisdom to gain. David's anointing, and sitting on the throne in Hebron, is just the beginning.

Many thought after Saul's death David would immediately become the King of a united Israel. It doesn't happen. Abner, Commander of the deceased King's army, hijacks the throne by controlling Saul's only surviving son, 40 year-old Ishbosheth. David's men are eager to unify the Nation, even to the extent of going to war. David, however, is neither upset nor disappointed. David knows there are obstacles to uniting the kingdom; now is not the time to force unification. It is then his nephews and others begin to realize in addition to the ever-increasing trust in God, it is obvious David is also learning to be more patient while putting into service God's plan. God has a plan for all of us; we must learn and accept there are no shortcuts in God's plans. His timetable, for each event on our narrow path, will prevail. Even the impetuous Joab, who is always ready to battle, concedes it is prudent to follow David's plan.

A year goes by and the armies of Abner and Joab encounter each other at the opposite sides of a pond in Gibeon. Spotting each other, Joab and Abner, both generals being true to nature, want to engage. Abner proposes he and Joab choose representatives to engage in a friendly contest, like a wrestling match; each side selecting twelve men. Evidently, neither side trusts the other for they all bring weapons, and all 24 men end up dead. A battle between the armies ensues; Joab's men are trouncing Abner's army and Abner flees on foot.

*"And the three sons of Zeruiah were there, Joab, and Abishai, and Asahel: and Asahel was as light of foot as a wild roe." (2 Samuel 2:18 ASV)* Asahel, swift on his feet, persistently pursues Abner; he covets the armor of a general, it's a magnificent trophy. Abner repeatedly and strongly advises Asahel to stop chasing him; Abner knows he is a far superior warrior than Asahel, even if he is slower at running. He suggests to Asahel, "Chase someone you have a chance to beat when you catch them." Tired of running and Asahel's dogged persistence convinces Abner he may as well stop. Abner stops, engages Asahel in a fight, and kills him. Joab and

Abishai continue the pursuit until dark at which time the chase ends.

The death of their baby brother plants a seed of hate in Joab and Abishai's hearts; the hatred is buried in them, but not forgotten. David loses another close confidante. Asahel, like Samuel, were persons with whom David felt comfortable discussing God. Asahel was one of the few persons who could rein in David, and coax him into refocusing on God. David has now lost two close friends, Asahel and Jonathan.

As a result of the battle at Gibeon, Israel's civil war begins; it's an impediment negatively impacting the prospects of Israel's unification. It will be 6 ½ years of combat between the armies of Hebron and Jerusalem before Israel is a united kingdom. Joab takes advantage of these years of war to build his own resources and reputation. He's creating his own power base within the army. He knows that his soldiers love and trust him, they consider him the ultimate leader, and will faithfully follow him into battle.

The situation is not as positive for General Abner. He is very concerned about the way the civil war is preceding. Abner is anxious about his personal welfare; it doesn't appear Saul's house is going to be able to serve his purpose much longer. Also, Abner is irate Ishbosheth had the audacity to raise-up in anger concerning his sexual relationship with Saul's concubine. He begins intimidating Ishbosheth, "Maybe it is true David is God's anointed." He repeatedly threatens to turn Saul's kingdom over to David, and ultimately he acts upon his traitorous threats. Abner secretly meets with King David. Twenty-two years ago these two first met when David killed Goliath and the General escorted the boy hero to King Saul. Now General Abner comes to King David, hat in hand, trying to ascertain what kind of deal he can cut for turning over Jerusalem's army, and the throne. Amongst David's stipulations is the return of his first wife, Michal, who is currently married to another man. David and Abner reach terms and come to an agreement; Abner departs.

David convened the clandestine meeting with Abner when he knew Joab would be out raiding villages. David wanted to have this meeting in secret to ensure Joab and Abjshai's hatred for Abner would not interfere with his kingdom building negotiations. Upon Joab's return to Hebron his allies inform him of Abner's visit and the surreptitious meeting he had with King David. Joab confronts David, "Why did you allow Abner to leave here alive?" Joab is not going to be satisfied with any reply David gives. Joab is angry but even more confused, "Why do you not feel about Abner killing Asahel as I do. You had a closer relationship with Asahel than you have with your own blood brothers." This is a benchmark turning point in their relationship. Their personal quests for power, and the aggressive and arrogant nature the pursuit of power fosters, is driving them further apart.

Joab orders some of his most trustworthy men to catch up to Abner, "Tell him the King wants to see him, and bring him back." Talking to Abishai, Joab wonders what kind of deal David agreed to with Abner; "Who did he throw under the bus!" Upon his men's return: *"Joab and Abishai his brother slew Abner, because he had killed their brother Asahel at Gibeon in the battle." (2 Samuel 3:30 ASV)* As this long awaited moment arrives, the outcomes David desired from the secret meeting mean absolutely nothing to Asahel's brothers. At this moment, what matters to them is their thirst for retribution is satiated. And as an added plus, Joab has eliminated any negotiations likely to have taken place for his War Counselor position.

Think about it though, did David really intend to replace Joab with Abner? How likely would it be that David even wanted Abner leading his army? Abner's resume indicates, as the General of Israel's Army, he failed to keep King Saul and his three sons alive. And, he is a traitor to King Ishbosheth. David being realistic understands Joab at this moment is his best choice.

David publically disavows any knowledge, participation, or complicity in Abner's death. David says he could not control Asahel's brothers, Joab and Abishai. To further convey sorrow and innocence, David plays a prominent role in Abner's funeral by reading the eulogy. At the repast David conspicuously does not partake in the food for he is fasting until sunset. While privately David is enjoying the revenge on Abner, he orchestrates a period of sorrow and grief for public consumption, including further distancing himself from that vile murderer, Joab. David's plan is to manage the situation in a more strategic manner, including his tacit consent to kill Abner. David is looking at the state of affairs from a King's perspective; his first obligation is to unite Israel; make it a stronger nation. David grieves for Asahel and is happy he is revenged, but he is installing unifying steps to foster the coming together of Israel; he's serving a larger purpose. Gary Greenberg in his book, *The Sins of King David*, describes a few of the ways people view King David: "history's first renaissance man, a diplomat of consummate skill, a politician of great wisdom."[6]

When King Ishobosheth, hears of Abner's death, he is petrified. The news rapidly flows through Jerusalem and the citizens are in fear and despair; General Abner the protector from their enemies is dead. So David derives another benefit from Abner's death; the people's fear for their safety and freedom. None have faith in King Ishobosheth's ability to protect them, nor do they respect his leadership. Two captains in Abner's army recognize these facts and decide to take advantage of the current leadership vacuum and seek fame and fortune. Their plan is to kill the King, and they do just that. They cut off his head and take it to King David in Hebron expecting accolades and rewards. They get neither; they get admonished and are told what happened to the Amalekite soldier who bragged about killing King Saul. David orders his men to kill and mutilate the two assassins. Another benefit is derived: Ishobosheth's death expedites David's quest to unify the throne.

# CHAPTER 9

# THE ARK OF THE COVENANT

*"SO THE PHILISTINES FOUGHT, AND THE ISRAELITES WERE DEFEATED AND EVERY MAN FLED TO HIS TENT.[11] THE ARK OF GOD WAS CAPTURED."*
*1 SAMUEL 4:16 (KJV)*

During this civil war the House of David grows stronger as The House of Saul weakens. The sons of Jacob acknowledge *they all are the tribes of Israel*, and they flock to Hebron, demanding David become their King. At 30 he became King of Judah, and now at 37, David and the tribes compose a covenant forming their relationship, which has obligations on all parties.

Twenty years ago people heard whispers that David had been anointed to become the next King; nearly all feel he has always been God's choice. Most heard of God's blessings when David was a renegade and eluding Saul's army. The adventurous tales kept alive the people's passion and love for David. David is looked upon as one of them; and in their minds he is still that pious shepherd boy at heart. Over time the people witness God's favor to David through the number of wives and concubines he acquires resulting in many daughters and 11 sons. Israelites believe sons are a measure of a man's relationship with God. David now has the power of a united kingdom behind him. He is starting to feel emboldened and entitled; he solidifies this power. David establishes a palace guard of mercenaries for his personal protection. And, he establishes his sons as Ministers. The journey to Kingship has been long and grueling; a significant benchmark has been reached; David is now ready to attack the nations surrounding Jerusalem and expand the Kingdom of Israel. Under King David's rule Israel's boundaries will increase from 6,000 to 60,000 square miles.

"Now David said, "Whoever attacks the Jebusites first shall be chief and captain." And Joab the son of Zeruiah went up first, and became chief." (1 Chronicles 11:6 NKJV) David now controls the stronghold of Zion and renames it the City of David. The City will become the center of Israel's Spiritual and political life. The extermination of the Jebusites serves as an opening for David and Joab to somewhat heal their differences. To them, defeating armies and conquering nations is cathartic. It's something they both are good at and take pleasure in doing. In their long and close relationship the two have been elevating themselves in their own minds. Their personal pride and selfish ambitions have placed a wedge between them. But even as David and Joab both privately surmise they may someday become opponents, they also recognize today their respective needs for each other. They basically agree, to disagree, on some issues.

King David begins uniting the Kingdom of Israel. In addition to conquering nations by war, a continued strategy for David is marriages to attain political alliances. Joab and Abishai frequently reminisce about David's marriage to Nabal's wife, Abigail, which provided him control of Camel and the wealth Abigail inherited. They consider that episode as the template of David's kingdom building strategy. At this time in history there is no one that has the political knowledge or military might of David, and he attributes this to God's guidance and favor.

Now that his kingship is established and the Kingdom is united, David decides the Ark of the Covenant should be returned. The ark is a symbol of the presence of God and even though it is located only eight miles away in Gath it has been gone from Jerusalem for over fifty years. The new King feels the City of David should be the center of Israel's Spiritual life, and the Ark of the Covenant must reside in the City. All the people are invited to partake in this glorious moment of bringing the ark back home. Along with the assembly, David, as a symbolic gesture, takes 30,000 of his best men to retrieve the ark; it's the same number of Israelite soldiers killed in the battle when the ark was lost a half century ago.

David plans for the return of the ark to be a victory celebration, a revival. After the caravan's eight mile walk, they retrieve the ark from the house of Abinadab, and the celebration begins. Various types of musical instruments are playing, dancing breaks out everywhere; the joy of celebrating with one another is exhilarating. The people believe Jehovah is truly with them again; He's not a fading memory. As a congregation, the Israelites have not collectively felt God's Spirit for many decades.

Then, the oxen stumble. Uzzah puts his hand on the ark to prevent it from falling and the error of touching the ark cost him his life. A ritual to properly transport the ark has been passed down through the generations. Ahithophel, one of David's Counselors, heard of the King's plan to return the Ark of the Covenant to

Jerusalem. He was appalled that the King did not consult anyone from the priesthood to plan this spiritual event, and to manage the logistics. Knowing the King's private plans beforehand, Ahithophel intentionally did not offer advice or give warning as to the appropriate protocol for transporting the ark. Ahithophel has an issue with the "sheep boy" who thinks he is closer to God than him. He felt David didn't have the proper respect for the priesthood.

David had good intentions but he lacked the knowledge of the priests. The crises angers and at the same time frightens David, he fears God is displeased. God took Uzzah's life and David is unsure if this punishment will extend to him and the people. David is not only anxious, he is mystified, *"How shall the ark of Jehovah come unto me?" (2 Samuel 6:9 ASV)* Abishai and Joab support David's quick improvisation, *"David would not remove the ark of Jehovah unto him into the city of David; but David carried it aside into the house of Obed-edom the Gittite." (2 Samuel 6:10 ASV)* Being disallowed the ark is constantly on David's mind, he is in despair but he has learned a valuable lesson; wait on an affirmative indication from God before proceeding.

Around the same time of the Ark of the Covenant debacle, the word of David becoming King of all Israel has spread across the region. Accolades come from Hiram, King of Tyre, who acknowledges David as the King of the united Israel. He demonstrates his friendship and allegiance by sending materials and craftsmen to build David a house. For the two Kings, this symbol of their relationship is more than a home for David and his family. The symbol visibly declares their alliance, and it is a strategic optic for their common enemy, the Philistines.

Conversely, when the Philistines hear of David being the King of a united Israel they are alarmed. In response they unite their armies; their goal is to strike before Judah and Jerusalem's armies unify. David goes into prayer asking, "God what shall I do. Should I fight?" God gives permission, and He provides strategies for the engagement. Joab is ecstatic to hear the affirmative orders particularly since he's now the General of Israel's united army. David continues his purge of Israel's enemies; he subdues the Philistines, and kills thousands of Syrians. David crushes and debilitates their armies to the point where they no longer can oppose the kingdom of Israel. As revenge for the Philistines taking the Ark of the Covenant David's army seize all the images the Philistines worship. David is God's punisher, he's God's sword against Israel's historical enemies.

Several months after the ark was left with Obed-Edom, Abishai reports to David how prosperous Obed-Edom has become, and David grows optimistic. He senses God is no longer angry and is speaking to him through Obed-Edom's abnormal opulence. David feels he now has God's permission to move the ark to The City of David. *"Then David said, "No one may carry the ark of God but the Levites, for the LORD has chosen them to carry the ark of God and to minister before Him forever."(1 Chronicles 15:2 NKJV).* David gathers Zadok, Abiathar, and the Levites together to instruct them, *"bring up the ark of the LORD God of Israel to the place I have prepared for it."* He again gathers the people of Israel. The celebration begins by worshiping God with burnt offerings of bulls and rams. Then the sounds of trumpets, stringed instruments, and songs of worship begin filling the air along with the offerings' rising smoke. David while energetically dancing exposes himself; everyone witnesses, including his wife Michal. When Michal meets up with David, she reproves him for acting like a common peasant, and rebukes his behavior as inappropriate in light of his royal status. Thereafter the two distance themselves from each other.

Even with the frightful death of Uzzah, and the estrangement of Michal, David's heart still overflows with gratitude. He enquires of Abishai *"Is there yet any that is left of the house of Saul, that I may show him kindness for Jonathan's sake?" (2 Samuel 9:1 ASV)* Abishai finds Ziba, Saul's land servant, who is happy to inform David that Mephibosheth, Jonathan's son, is still alive years after Jonathan and Saul's deaths. David greets Mephibosheth, assures him of his safety, returns his family's wealth to him, and then invites him to eat at the King's table for the rest of his life.

The blessing of bringing the ark back to Jerusalem boosts David's passion to the extent that he wants to build, "a permanent residence for the Lord who lives in tents." David feels since now there is peace in a united Israel this is a good time for the people to show God their gratitude. He speaks to his priest, Nathan, who David considers a friend as well as his Spiritual Counselor. Nathan is initially enthusiastic about building a house for God, but when the Lord and Nathan have their evening chat Nathan is admonished, and given different instructions. David's transgressions preclude him building the Ark of the Covenant's Sanctuary. God wants David to focus on building his dynasty.

Nathan tells David "God eventually will provide an heir that shall build a permanent residence for the Ark of the Covenant." *"And thine house and thy kingdom shall be established for ever before thee: thy throne shall be established forever." (2 Samuel 7:16 KJV) The Bible Commentary* by Jamieson-Fausset-Brown says, "It is customary for the *oldest son born after the father's succession to the throne* to succeed him in his dignity as king"[7]. David had several sons by wives and concubine that were born in Hebron and in Jerusalem. *The Bible Commentary* by Jamieson-Fausset-Brown also says, "But by a special ordinance and promise of God, his successor was to be a son born after this time; and the departure from the established method of the East in fixing the succession, can be accounted for on no other known ground, except the fulfill-ment of the Divine promise".[8] Even though the unborn Solomon will not be David's oldest son, God ordained Solomon to be the next king and the heir to build His house. God's will, will prevail.

David reads between the lines. He is prohibited from building God's house, but David feels he is permitted to purchase build-ing materials and identify the craftsmen that his heir will need, and he proceeds accordingly. Despite God's piercing reason for denying him to build His house, David feels Blessed. He visits the Ark of the Covenant as God's servant to give praise and worship. He is pleased and appreciative for what God has ordained. David humbly enters God's assigned tent and while sitting before the ark begins prayers of thanksgiving. One prayer of thanks is for the Nation of Israeli being established: David is the King and Judge, Zadok is the High Priest, David's sons are Chief Ministers, and Joab is the Commander of Israel's army. As he has done most of his life, David marvels, *"Who am I, O Lord Jehovah, and what is my house that thou hast brought me thus far?" (2 Samuel 7:18 ASV)*

When the King of Ammon dies David sends a special envoy to offer his condolences to support the King's son Hanun. Many people across the land are uncertain about his temperament of the all-powerful King David, and are leery of the intentions. King Hanun is persuaded by his princes that David cannot be trusted; that he's sending people as spies to assess their strengths and weaknesses. Hanun is convinced and boldly shows his distrust and contempt for David. He orders the humiliation of David's envoys, by shaving their beards and cutting their clothes; exposing their bodies. It's a declaration of war. *"And it was told David; and he gathered all Israel together, and passed over the Jordan, and came to Helam." (2 Samuel 10:17 ASV)*

# CHAPTER 10

# SELF PRESERVATION

*"AND IT CAME TO PASS, AFTER THE YEAR WAS EXPIRED, AT THE TIME WHEN KINGS GO FORTH TO BATTLE, THAT DAVID SENT JOAB, AND HIS SERVANTS WITH HIM, AND ALL ISRAEL; AND THEY DESTROYED THE CHILDREN OF AMMON, AND BESIEGED RABBAH. BUT DAVID TARRIED STILL AT JERUSALEM."*

*2 SAMUEL 11:1 (KJV)*

With winter setting in Joab decides to remain in Helam, and utilize these months to prepare for the spring assault on the Ammonites.  This is a successful era in Israel's history; they are united, their territory is expanding, prosperity abounds, and they are finally at peace.  But even though there is peace, they are always looking to expand the Kingdom by conquering additional territories.  Spring is a long-established starting period for military operations; the spring months provide dry passable roads making travel to and from war zones less difficult.  This particular spring the plan is for Israel's mighty army to destroy the Ammonites as revenge for their assault on the King's ambassadors.

Spring arrives; the army begins the long trek south through the wilderness on the north-side of Rabbah. Along the way they encounter over ten thousands Syrian mercenaries, and extinguish them. Next, they exterminate the population living in the villages that surround Rabbah's countryside. And now with the city isolated, they attack Rabbah's walled metropolis. Abishai comments to Joab, "It doesn't appear our King has any interest in this war; I've noticed lately he hardly ever leaves the city. Joab's response, "Our King has become more settled since he has taken the throne, he's become too comfortable. It's fortunate he still has us, and this dedicated army, to keep the Kingdom strong, safe, and prosperous."

Meanwhile back at the King's quarters David awakes from a late afternoon nap. He decides to stroll on his flat-roofed terrace to get some cool evening air. Walking along the rooftop he spies a beautiful woman bathing. For David, conquests in wars have lost their excitement, yet the boredom without military engagements is tortuous. But this exhilaration that David feels in his heart right now brings fond memories of other conquests; he is stimulated, and he impulsively reacts to his feelings.

*"And David sends and inquired after the woman. And one said, Is not this Bath-sheba, the daughter of Eliam, the wife of Uriah the Hittite?" (2 Samuel 11:3 ASV)* You would suppose only a prominent family would reside in the palace's neighborhood, especially next door. Being his next door neighbor, one would imagine David knew Eliam who is also one of his Men of Valor. Additionally, Eliam is the son of Ahithophel, who is Bathsheba's grandfather. Did David also know Uriah? Like his father in-law, Uriah is one of David's elite mighty men, a member of The Thirty. One thing David knew for sure: Uriah is in Rabbah with Joab.

Ignoring the obvious warnings signals, David sends his personal guards for Bathsheba. The King's guards arrive at her door with orders she does not understand. *Did something happen to Uriah?* Upon arrival she hears nothing about her husband's welfare but quickly understands why her presence was demanded. David has his way with her, and sends her back home. As soon as Bathsheba arrives she orders two of her servants to prepare for travel, they are going to her grandfather's house. The dislike Ahithophel has for David turns to hatred when he hears of the assault on his granddaughter. He comforts and counsels her. He advises her to look out for her own welfare; "You are well aware you can't trust the King. I will speak to my close friends about this matter and we will support and protect you. Return home and wait to hear from me."

After Bathsheba leaves Ahithophel decides to visit Nathan, David's priest and personal counsel; he informs him of what transpired. Nathan and Ahithophel are brothers of the priesthood and have a long-standing relationship. Ahithophel convinces Nathan that Bathsheba is a victim. He asks Nathan to watch over Bathsheba and Nathan vows his commitment.

*"And the woman conceived; and she sent and told David, and said, I am with child".* (2 Samuel 11:5 ASV) David took his eye off God; he did not turn away from temptation even when his servant warned who Bathsheba is, and who comprised her family. David still has no intention of taking this mess to God, which contradicts and ignores his past behavior when faced with difficult, consequential decisions. Just like us, David is trying to hide his sinful acts from God. It's gotten to the point he's ashamed to go to God. It is remarkable that in the midst of sin, and during its cover up, we stop acknowledging God sees everything. God knows. Go to Him with it. The sooner the better; He's waiting!

But "The man after God's own heart" persists down the slippery slope of sin. David decides to figure this out himself; he devises a plan to make Uriah culpable and the cover-up begins. David sends his personal servant with a message to Joab with instructions for Uriah to report to the King without delay; David did not offer a reason.  Upon receiving the message Joab tells Abishai to find Uriah and inform him he is to report to the King immediately.  The brothers wonder what could be so important to pull one of their leaders off the battle field.

Uriah's mind is racing on the way to the palace; *what could the King personally want of me. David is always scheming. Did I do something wrong? I'm apprehensive about meeting him.*  King David and Uriah meet.  David starts and ends with small talk about Rabbah, never explaining why Uriah is there.  David finally says to Uriah, *"Go down to thy house, and wash thy feet. And Uriah departed out of the king's house, and there followed him a mess of food from the king. ("2 Samuel 11:8 ASV)* The King has set his trap: Uriah is to lay with his already pregnant wife, so Bathsheba's baby will be considered his.

For many years Uriah has witnessed David use smoke and mirrors on those of whom he has bad intentions.  Uriah ponders, *David talking to me about Rabbah's progress is uncharacteristic of him; we've never personally talked about conflicts. I've been called away from battle for four days, and I have not been told why; so suspicious.  David is purpose-driven, always precise, meticulous, and to the point, so what's going on?* Uriah does not yet know the subterfuge, but he correctly suspects it is not to his benefit.

Since Bathsheba's midnight visit, the palace personnel have not been able to stop talking about her sudden and quick visit to the palace.  They are well aware of whom Bathsheba is, she has attended many of the King's gatherings with her husband.  So when it's heard Uriah is in the palace, the word of his arrival spreads like wildfire; particularly amongst the household staff, and the King's guards. *Why is Uriah here? Does he know Bathsheba was recently here?* And to further confuse the situation, that evening they discover Uriah sleeping *"at the door of the king's house with all the servants of his lord, and went not down to his house." (2 Samuel 11:9 ASV)* Respectfully, the servants ask "Why are you here at the palace?" but Uriah did not have an answer, he was trying to figure out the same thing himself.

When David finds out that Uriah had spent the night on the grounds with the servants he is disappointed, angry, and perplexed. He asks Uriah, why? Uriah laid out many reasons why he could not indulge himself: loyalty to his King, to his country, and to his comrades who are right now engaged in battle. Uriah's expressions of loyalty did not prick David's heart. David's heart has been hardened and his mind is being controlled by the cover up. David hasn't looked into the face of his Lord lately. God would help David to realize that bad intentions that lead to sinful followup actions are unacceptable.

David tells Uriah to hang around for a few days and he'll get back to him; David figures this will allow more time for Uriah's appetite for the pleasures of life to quicken. Uriah still does not understand why he has been taken from his post. Three days of fellowship with the servants leads them to divulging what they know to be the truth: "The King's personal guards brought Bathsheba to the King's quarters." With this revelation Uriah finally understands what's going on; he believes it; he knows David's habits and history. What is most important now is for Uriah not to confront David, because it would be suicide. He's aware that something bad invariably happens to the husbands of the wives whom David covets. Uriah is not shocked, but disappointed. He has been with David long enough to have witnessed David "acquire" other men's wives; he just didn't think David would do that to him.

David invites Uriah to dinner; another desperate attempt to entice Uriah to lay with Bathsheba: *"And when David had called him, he did eat and drink before him; and he made him drunk: and at even he went out to lie on his bed with the servants of his lord, but went not down to his house."* *(2 Samuel 11:13 ASV)* Believing his life is in danger keeps Uriah sober enough not to succumb to the flesh.

Hearing of Uriah sleeping with the servants again makes David furious and paranoid. David continues to make decisions without God's input. He writes a letter to Joab with instructions on how Uriah should be killed; it's an order to kill one of The Thirty with no reason given. David hands Uriah his own death sentence to deliver to Joab. Uriah has a long ride back to Rabbah; his mind is racing: *Is Bathsheba ok? What's in this letter? Should I tell Joab what David did? Will Joab have mercy on me?*

Joab sees Uriah riding towards him, he smiles, and glad to see he's ok but still curious as to why he had to go see the King in the first place. After greeting each other Uriah presents the letter. The letter visibly changes Joab's demeanor and he immediately calls for Abishai. Abishai reads the letter and tells Uriah to join his troops. The two brothers are in disbelief; why would David want Uriah dead. Was he a traitor? They didn't believe that of Uriah, and if so, why try to disguise his death in a battle; what's the secret?

Joab sends Abishai to the City of David to find out what is the truth. They know David better than most; something is not right. Abishai conducts his investigation talking with the King's servants as well as the soldiers who remained behind to protect the King. Upon his return, Abishai shares the information with Joab emphasizing, "The servants told Uriah what happened to Bathsheba, and they were adamant Uriah never saw Bathsheba while he was

there, even though the King explicitly encouraged him to do so."
They both arrived at the same conclusion as Uriah, David betrayed
Uriah.  Joab and Abishai stare at each other with one question in
mind, what do we do now?

Their thinking is, *killing Uriah for David's reasons is crossing
the line.  Uriah is one of us, a brother warrior.*  But putting that
emotion aside, not killing Uriah meant taking on David, which was
not an option.  Joab did not believe the army would follow him to
overthrow David.  This is the moment their mindset about David
had finally changed; the straw has broken the camel's back.  They
had long ago taken him off a pedestal, but now they no longer
can convince themselves that David at least has got their back.
Regrettably they both know Uriah must die and many good soldiers will die as part of this conspiracy.  But, on the positive side,
they feel they have a weapon against David; an indictment of him
not being loyal or honorable to his men in the army.  Joab now
possesses facts of which he knows David would not want the army
to be aware.  *"And it came to pass, when Joab kept watch upon
the city, that he assigned Uriah unto the place where he knew that
valiant men were.  And the men of the city went out, and fought
with Joab: and there fell some of the people, even of the servants
of David; and Uriah the Hittite died also." (2 Samuel 11:16-17 ASV)*
Uriah is killed by an archer's arrow, shot from atop the city wall.

Joab sends a messenger who describes the battle to the King.
David is furious Joab would take such risks and lose so many in
the fight.  David becomes composed when he hears, *"Uriah the
Hittite died also." "Then David said unto the messenger, Thus shalt
thou say unto Joab, Let not this thing displease thee, for the sword
devoureth one as well as another." (2 Samuel 11:25 ASV)* David
also recognizes Joab implemented a plan different than the one
he suggested; noticeably a better plan.  Since the death of Abner,

David and Joab's leeriness of each other's motives has exacerbated. David notices Joab's frequent disobedience, and how he is increasingly making independent decisions. David is not happy about it, but David realizes he has drastically compromised his position by his knowing a loyal warrior's wife, and afterward, having the warrior killed. It's not a good time to confront Joab.

Abishai has now witnessed what Joab has been saying for many years, "David is changing. He has become more self-righteous; he's less considerate of others." Living on the "East Side" has its traps; it's all milk and honey. The traps that come with absolute power are fraught with alluring temptations for every person including God's beloved. At this time in his life David refuses to discuss these entrapments with God; he's still handling matters himself.

Ahithophel sadly informs Bathsheba of Uriah getting killed in battle. He had no details at the time but he had suspicions. *"And when the wife of Uriah heard that Uriah her husband was dead, she made lamentation for her husband." (2 Samuel 11:26 ASV)* The mourning period passes and David sends for Bathsheba, no lamentation for him. David marries Bathsheba, and their child is born. David feels all is well now! Other than some concern that Joab and Abishai may have their suspicions, he thinks nobody knows. *"But the thing that David had done displeased Jehovah." (2 Samuel 11:27 ASV)*

# CHAPTER 11

# RETURNING TO JEHOVAH

## "AND DAVID SAID UNTO NATHAN, I HAVE SINNED AGAINST THE LORD"
### 2 SAMUEL 12:13A (KJV)

For almost a year Nathan has personally investigated the grave situation involving King David, the pregnant Bathsheba, and the death of Uriah. Nathan has talked to the servants, the palace guards, and particularly with Gad the Prophet who has a close relationship with David. David respects Gad's counsel because of the prudent advice given during his fugitive years. Nathan has also spoken with David's nephew, Abishai, inquiring what he discovered during his investigation. And of course he frequently meets Ahithophel who had informed him of the abuse, and subsequently notified him of Bathsheba being with child. Nathan and Ahithophel's relationship goes back many years as King David's advisors; they have a bond. They've had many confidential talks since David's crowning, mostly to discuss the common interest of preserving a strong and prominent clergy. But the specific Voice Nathan is waiting for has not yet been heard. Up until that point, the palace's occupants felt nothing would happen to the King for his assault on Bathsheba or the suspicious death of Uriah. Everyone agreed David is not the type of person you confront with accusations without putting your life at risk.

After an exhaustive investigation Nathan has a strong opinion as to what happened, but his challenge is how to forthrightly and safely confront David with his findings. Finally, late one evening the Lord visits Nathan. The visit results in Nathan being convinced he must stop procrastinating and persuade David to confess his multiple sins involving Bathsheba and Uriah.

The next morning before dawn Gad the Prophet arrives at Nathan's house. He finds Nathan very distraught, pacing the floor. There is no question in Gad's mind that Yahweh has visited; he has seen responses to His visits before, but never has any been this severe. Nathan tells Gad of his difficult assignment, and asks him to walk with him to the palace. The sun is just rising when they leave. Now aware of Nathan's challenging assignment Gad nervously asks, "Won't it seem strange us going to the palace this early?" Nathan, trying to show confidence assures him, "Not at all, I arrive unannounced at any time in my role as David's Spiritual Counselor."

Nathan has been ordered to remind David no man is above sin nor is anyone sinless, even him. Nathan knows better than most that David does not take kindly to admonishment. He is resolute to be obedient to God despite his fear. He shares his concern, "Gad, its imperative I deliver God's message in a truthful and effective manner, and at the same time, in a safe way." Gad assures Nathan that the correct person was selected for this assignment. He reminds Nathan, "You and King David have developed a brotherly relationship over the years. But Nathan, what you really have going for you: David knows if you say God sent the message; God sent the message."

As they are walking God provides Nathan a parable to tell David of a selfish, powerful man taking advantage of a poor man, (2 Samuel 12:1-4). Nathan delivers the parable and David becomes indignant and judgmental: *"And David's anger was greatly kindled against the man; and he said to Nathan, As Jehovah liveth, the man that hath done this is worthy to die." (2 Samuel 12:5 ASV)* Visibly nervous, *"Nathan said to David, Thou art the man." (2 Samuel 12:7 ASV)* David is momentarily stunned and speechless; he knows Nathan hasn't the courage to accuse him unless commanded by Jehovah. Plus, he is clearly experiencing that *I gotcha moment*.

Before David can speak, God reminds him of how much he has done for him, and He would have done even more. God asks why David despised Him enough to do evil in His sight. David is told troubles will never depart from his house and adversity against him will come from within his household. *"For thou didst it secretly: but I will do this thing before all Israel, and before the sun." (2 Samuel 12:12 ASV)* It's an awakening for David. The stewardship of the throne, ordained for his unborn heir that was entrusted to him; he put it in danger. David sinks deep into prayer; he confesses his sin, and asks for forgiveness. Nathan tells him God has put his transgressions behind Him and David will not die. But the child shall die because of David's deeds.

At which time Nathan happily departs. Briskly walking on the way home he and Gad are relieved that David humbly accepted God's words. Gad confesses, "I was nervous the whole time." They laugh about the difference in their feelings walking back to Nathan's house compared to the somber mood on the way to the palace. Nathan implores Gad, "Stay close to David, he considers you a friend with wisdom; be a comforter and supporter." Nathan knows David will be experiencing some very difficult times now and in the future.

The baby boy becomes sick. David pleads for mercy and goes into a period of mourning knowing well the boy is going to die; God said so. David fasts, he wears ashes and sackcloth, he's remorseful for causing the child's death, and he continues to pray for a miracle. Seven days later the child dies. Afraid, the servants don't reveal the child's death, but David notices them whispering and he asks if the child has died. David accepts their affirmative answer; he gets up and bathes, worships, and then eats a meal. The confused servants are told once God's verdict was fulfilled it was time to move on. God blesses Bathsheba and David with another child, they name him Solomon. God is pleased with Solomon's birth. God chooses Solomon to be the next King of Israel. David feels that God has forgiven him; but he is quite sure his punishment shall continue.

Realizing there are changes coming in the royal household, the shrewd Nathan decides his security and future depends on his relationship with Israel's next ruler. Aligning himself with that person provides his only chance of retaining leadership of the clergy. Being privy to inside information, Nathan bets on Bathsheba and Solomon. He personally takes over the education of Solomon and becomes his mentor.

Back at Rabbah, the two year war with the Ammonites has come to an end with the capture of the city. Joab sends word to David that they will be marching into Rabbah. The brothers have recently heard of God's reprimand of David for assassinating Uriah; Joab is pleased and encouraged. This is the first time he recalls God severely punishing David. Joab is sure he is now more suited to lead than David.  Joab feels he is a better warrior, if God is no longer on David's side.  The brothers have witnessed many times God showing David Favor; they feel God is David's only advantage over them.  (Interestingly, the brothers are correct.  David's positive relationship with God is what sets Joab and David apart.) Abishai has frequently enquired of Nathan why God loves David so much, constantly protecting him from harm, and forgiving him when he sins.  Nathan replies, "God continuously loves David, as He does us all, because of grace.  Our deeds, good or bad, do not order His love." Joab has always been resentful of David and God's relationship.  Their motives for wanting a relationship with God are quite different; Joab wishes for an association with God because of what God can do for him, and David desires a relationship with God because of Who He is.

David arrives at Rabbah in time to divide the spoils of war, and take retribution on the Ammonite leaders that humiliated his Ambassadors.  Away from the palace, David reflects on the wayward path he has been on these past two years; difficult and painful years.  God's words keep haunting him: *"Now therefore the sword shall never depart from thy house, because thou hast despised me." (2 Samuel 12:10 ASV)*

# CHAPTER 12

# ATONEMENT PERSISTS AFTER FORGIVENESS

*"THUS SAITH JEHOVAH, BEHOLD, I WILL RAISE UP EVIL AGAINST THEE OUT OF THINE OWN HOUSE."*
                              *2 SAMUEL 12:11 (ASV)*

The cost for David's transgressions continues. His oldest son, Amnon, lusts for his half sister Tamar, exclaiming he loves her. He is getting himself overly worked up about the subject and it's affecting his health. His scheming cousin, Jonadab, becomes aware of his illness and asks, "What is the cause?" Hearing Amnon's reason Jonadab suggests how he can trick Tamar into laying with him. Amnon takes this risky advice while knowing Tamar is a virgin and the King is saving her to marry someone with wealth and power. He deceives his father by feigning sickness, *"Amnon said unto the king, Let his sister Tamar come, I pray thee, and make me a couple of cakes in my sight that I may eat from her hand." (2 Samuel 13:6 ASV)* The King consents and Tamar prepares the cakes for Amnon. When she brings the cakes to him, Amnon dismisses his servants and suggests Tamar lay with him.  She refuses; she beseeches him, and through tears details several reasons why it's wrong and will be harmful to both of them.  Amnon forces her to bed, ignoring her pleas of reason and tears of sorrow.  Expecting her to express satisfaction, Tamar's negative response, and her resistance, angers Amnon.  He dismisses her, throws her out the house, and locks the door.  Being disgraced and ashamed Tamar covers herself with ashes, and rips her colorful robe.  She goes to her brother Absalom's house where she remains a scorned woman.  Absalom hates Amnon for the assault on his sister but never speaks of it; he tells Tamar, "Don't mention this to anyone." Absalom plans to get revenge at the appropriate time.  David finds out what Amnon did to Tamar and is very angry but does nothing about it.  Perhaps David realizes the hypocrisy of him giving advice; he may be constricted by the guilt of his own amoral behavior.  Absalom considers his father's inaction as an explicit acceptance of this despicable assault on his own daughter.  Now Absalom's hatred is directed towards both his father and Amnon.

Two years pass and Absalom sees his opportunity to kill Amnon.  He invites his father and his sons to the annual sheep shearing celebration.  David passes on the invitation, which Absalom expected and desired.  He persuades his father to let all his sons attend the festival.  Absalom then explains the actual plan to his servants, "You are attending the celebration with me; while there you shall kill my brother, Amnon.  I assure you, there will be no repercussions towards you." During the celebration Absalom sees Amnon feasting with his brothers and he signals his servants to kill him.  Witnessing the murder, Amnon's brothers are horrified; thinking they are to be next, they quickly flee and escape.  Amnon's death is revenge for his sister, but Absalom is not finished; he is determined to punish his father.  He now believes it will benefit him being the heir to the throne when he takes his father's crown.

When the news first gets to David he is misinformed that all of his sons were killed by Absalom's servants; he is devastated. His nephew Jonadab arrives later and reports only his oldest son Amnon is dead, which is of some relief to David (Jonadab does not share his complicity in this matter). Absalom flees to his grandfather King Talmai in Geshur, and remains there for three years.

After a couple of years, David who still mourns his son, Amnon, begins to long for his son Absalom.

Joab tells Abishai, "Recently I have had several meetings with David, at which time he keeps bringing up his longing for Absalom." They decide: *David's yearning for his son may be well-suited to address our plan to exit the King's service.* They know Absalom is still seething about his father's callous response to Tamar's assault. In their discussion the two brothers surmise: "Absalom could be an ally, and we would have more control if he was King. Absalom must realize he cannot seize the throne without our support." They proceed with the first step of the new strategy.

*"And Joab sent to Tekoa and brought from there a wise woman, and said to her, "Please pretend to be a mourner. "So Joab put the words in her mouth." (2 Samuel 14:2-3 NKJV)* Joab suggests telling David a bogus story about her family's feud hoping David will empathize and commit to intercede. Pleading for a ruling, she tells King David, "My family's dispute has taken one of my two sons and now the argument is on the verge of taking my last heir." Similar to when David raged about the rich man taking the poor man's lamb, promising retribution, he angrily promises the wise woman, *"As surely as the LORD lives," he said, "not one hair of your son's head will fall to the ground." (2 Samuel 14:11b NKJV)* Now that David is hooked, she tells him the truth. *The King asked, "Isn't the hand*

*of Joab with you in all this?" (Samuel14:19 NKJV)* David admits to himself, Joab can be a very able ally or a formidable adversary.

David is unaware of the real reason Joab is so eager for him to rekindle his relationship with Absalom. He doesn't care; David has been looking for an excuse. The King has been rationalizing, "The people will be relieved; there must be nationwide apprehension regarding who succeeds me to the throne; it's a valid fear." He gives permission for Joab to bring Absalom to the city where he and his family may reside with the stern provision Absalom does not meet with his father.

The years Absalom spent in Geshur produced three sons, and a daughter who is named after his sister, Tamar. Absalom has been fertile as a family man in those years but not fruitful in his quest to be King. It has been five years since he has seen his father. He feels living in the City of David, while at the same time being banned from seeing his father, has been a wasted two years. Joab has been appointed the designated liaison to his father. Unsuccessful attempts to reach Joab prompt Absalom to burn down one of his crop fields to get his attention, and Joab immediately responds. Absalom sends an ultimatum to his father, "Exonerate me or kill me, but do it to my face!" *"So Joab went to the king and told him. And when he had called for Absalom, he came to the king and bowed himself on his face to the ground before the king. Then the king kissed Absalom". (2 Samuel 14:33 NKJV)*

Competing parties detect a weakness in the Kingdom. These factions are jockeying for their preferred positions; each playing their games. At this point, Joab and Abishai don't know if their future will be with David or Absalom, they don't really care. They are sure they will have a role with the victor, and will wait patiently to see who that is.

Back in good standing with Dad, Absalom actively pursues his ambition to be King. Absalom decides to publicize the fact he is the oldest son, heir to the throne. Already known for his flamboyance, good looks, and long flowing hair, Absalom further lavishes himself with, *"chariots and horses, and fifty men to run before him." (2 Samuel 15:1 KJV)* Absalom is not willing to wait until the crown will traditionally pass on to the heir.

Absalom listens to the people's deep concern about King David's intentions to centralize government, his plan to take judicial power away from the local villages, and on top of that, the King proposes to raise their taxes. Absalom ingratiates himself to them by empathizing with their sorrows and concerns while at the same time making it obvious to them the King has not assigned anyone to hear their grievances. *Now Absalom would rise early and stand beside the way to the gate." (2 Samuel 15:2 NKJV)* Early each morning Absalom would meet as many as possible *"on the way to the gate"*. He listens to their woes and incessantly sympathizes with the people saying, "If only I was appointed a Judge *I could meet with you at the gate* and lessen your hardships." The ritual continues for four years with the number of his followers increasing because of the personal attention he bestows upon them. During these years Absalom exploits the people's dissatisfaction with the encroaching government. He paints a vivid and positive depiction of how he would rule differently on behalf of the multitude. Absalom is truly his father's son.

*Absalom says to his father, "I pray thee, let me go and pay my vow, which I have vowed unto the LORD, in Hebron." (2 Samuel 15:7 KJV)* Hebron is Absalom's birthplace where he knows he will be well received. David gives him permission to honor his "vow committed to the Lord." Absalom's vow is an excuse to go to Hebron to continue growing his followers. From Hebron Absalom sends *"spies"* throughout the nation to drum up commitments to his candidacy as King. The spies notify the Israelites: "When you hear the sound of the trumpet it's a sign Absalom is now Hebron's ruler." Absalom invites 200 of Israel's renowned leaders, to Hebron. The eyewitnesses don't know they are being used to legitimize the coup attempt. It is intended they be perceived as supporters of Absalom's rebellion, or if the crowning does not go as planned, they can be held as hostages.

Absalom sends for Ahithophel, David's esteemed Counselor who Absalom respects for his insight, not necessarily for his relationship to God. Absalom is sure that Ahithophel will welcome an opportunity to strike a painful blow to the King. Absalom, as well as many others, are fully aware Ahithophel despises David. The assault on his granddaughter, and making her a widow, exacerbated the oracle's hatred of David. It's a matter never to be forgotten or forgiven. The two conspire how to overthrow King David.

As time moves on, Absalom's followers are continuing to grow rapidly. And finally the sound of trumpets is being heard in Judah, indicating Absalom is King of Hebron. David has been keeping in close touch with his allies in Hebron so not to be caught by surprise. One consideration for David leaving is his concern that a battle could destroy the beautiful City of David. And to maintain a claim on the City, he intends to leave his concubine behind to manage the palace.

David gets word, *"The hearts of the men of Israel are after Absalom." (2 Samuel 15:13 KJV)* Upon being notified that strong talk of an attack is being discussed, David executes his evacuation plan to rapidly retreat beyond the Jordan River. Without delay he mobilizes his servants and family to vacate the City. The escape route will be a difficult task for the King, his family, staff, and servants. It's over 100 miles to the Jordan; a long walk, up and down hills, and over very difficult terrain. For Joab, and his well traveled army, this trip would normally be business as usual. But they had to uproot their families, and their belongings, for fear of both being captured and lost. This is a humiliating and exhausting experience for the King's royal family, and his entourage.

David's allies, who have sworn allegiance, march with him reaffirming their commitment. Zadok and all the Levites come along and bring the Ark of the Covenant. David's reflections of past Divine experiences bolster his faith that God will still be with him through this precarious moment. David feels God will return him to his rightful position on the throne. Holding strong to that faith, he instructs Zadok to return the ark to the city. Additionally he orders Zadok and Abiathar, "While in the city, spy on the enemy and send me messages by way of your sons."

David has heard Ahithophel joined Absalom; David prays that God will render Ahithophel's advice to Absalom worthless. David and Ahithophel have long had their differences; David thought of him as a man of intelligence, but he also felt Ahithophel was not filled with God's wisdom. When they arrive at the Mount of Olives, David climbs up the hill barefoot with ashes on his head, as a sign of his repentance. Arriving at the top he meets Hushai the Arkhite, the *King's Friend*[9]. They weave a scheme: *Hushai will join Absalom to argue against whatever advice Ahithophel proposes.* David knows Ahithophel will give Absalom sage advice. He instructs Hushai, "Any news is to be relayed to Zadok and Abiathar, and they will forward it to me."

David and the caravan descend down the mountain. Continuing a short distance David encounters Ziba, Saul's grandson's servant. Ziba was a crafty person who knew it was time to choose sides in this attempted coup. He chooses David; so he loaded up supplies and brings transportation for David's household. David asks the whereabouts of Mephibosheth and he is told upsetting news;

Mephibosheth is staying in the City. Mephibosheth is telling people, *"Today shall the house of Israel restore me the kingdom of my father."* *(2 Samuel 16:3 KJV)* In response to Mephibosheth's public disloyalty and ingratitude, David strips him of all his wealth and gives it to Ziba. Ziba humbles himself to David and gives thanks for showing him such favor.

At this time David is suspicious of everyone, but he accepts Ziba's report as truth because Ziba is showing his commitment. Under David's present situation, the major question, and his greatest worry, is Joab's commitment. However, right now, David must keep the faith because *"At this moment I need Joab should a war erupt with Absalom."*

There are many others in Israel that still love King Saul and hate King David. They believe David is not the type of person he purports to be. One of those doubters is Shimei the son of Gera. When the escaping caravan arrives at Shemei's hometown, Bahurim, he throws stones at David while continually cursing him, *"The LORD has brought upon you all the blood of the house of Saul. So, now you are caught in your own evil, because you are a bloodthirsty man!"* *(2 Samuel 16:8 NKJV)* Abishai strenuously objects to David allowing Shemei to curse the King and he offers to cut off his head. At this time David looks at Shemei as a minor problem compared to the challenge he has from his own flesh and blood. He orders Abishai to ignore him. David gets it; he will be under the Lord's judgment and His chastisement for an unspecified period. Shemei's actions may be a part of that penance. David speaks of Shemei's actions positively, *"It may be that the LORD will look on my affliction, and that the LORD will repay me with good for his cursing this day."* *(2 Samuel 16:13 NKV)*

# CHAPTER 13

# A HOUSE DIVIDED

*"FOR YOU DID IT SECRETLY, BUT I WILL DO THIS THING BEFORE ALL ISRAEL, BEFORE THE SUN."*
                                    *2 SAMUEL 12:12 (NKJV)*

An alliance between Ahithophel and Absalom presents a personal conflict for Ahithophel. He realizes Absalom becoming King could be an obstacle for his great-grandson's ascendance to the throne as prophesized. Ahithophel must decide; he prays, meditates, and concludes, "Solomon becoming King is Providential and will be a reality in the future, but the pleasure of finally getting revenge on David is at hand, which I will not let pass by!"

Absalom and his "army" enters the City of David. Riding close behind him is Ahithophel, a man who is known for his grumpy disposition yet surprisingly today he appears to be joyful. Finally, revenge for Ahithophel seems within reach. David's selfish assault on Bathsheba damaged Ahithophel's family legacy, and elevated his hatred towards the King. His merry mood suddenly changes when Hushai the Arkite shows up cunningly hailing Absalom as the King. Ahithophel is immediately suspicious. He and Hushai were peers who both advised the King. Even though Hushai was personally closer to David, Ahithophel considered himself the superior of the two Oracles. *"So Absalom said to Hushai, "Is this your loyalty to your friend? Why did you not go with your friend?"* Hushai explains, *"I follow who God and the people choose, and because I have served the father faithfully for years why not provide this experience and wisdom to the son." (2 Samuel 16:17-19 NKJV)* The answer gratifies Absalom's ego; *here's another of the King's advisors desiring to be my consultant.* He appoints Hushai as one of his Counselor.

Being content with Hushai's explanation Absalom dismisses him and turns to Ahithophel to privately discuss the next tactical moves. Ahithophel looks at this privilege to determine David's fate as a gift from God. He realizes by now David has figured out he has betrayed him. He also understands perfectly, if David doesn't die, no question he will. Ahithophel must convince Absalom to move quickly. But even before that, he must ensure Absalom's commitment to the coup is unshakable. He recalls Nathan's prophecy, *"Thus says the LORD: 'Behold, I will raise up adversity against you from your own house; and I will take your wives before your eyes and give them to your neighbor, and he shall lie with your wives in the sight of this sun." (2 Samuel 12:11 NKJV)*

Ahithophel loves the prophecy's irony. He convinces himself that God's decree for a public reprimand of David has been entrusted to him as justice for his family's harm and embarrassment. Ahithophel advises Absalom, *"Go in to your father's concubines, whom he has left to keep the house; and all Israel will hear that you are abhorred by your father, then shall the hands of all that are with thee shall be strong." (2 Samuel 16:21 NKJV)* Absalom is persuaded and acts upon his Counselor's advice. Ahithophel witnesses Absalom's public offense to the King, and delights in the royal family's public humiliation; it is extremely gratifying. He's also pleased with Absalom's public display of disrespect and insurrection. This ensures he cannot renege on his pledge to seize the throne.

Now comforted, Ahithophel stresses to Absalom the urgency of completing the coup without further delay. He emphasizes, "David will regroup very soon. Your father unquestionably has been spending a considerable amount of time with God throughout this ordeal. And, I am convinced when the King decides to respond it will be vigorous and decisive. Your Highness, it is imperative you take action before he decides." Ahithophel asks for consent to lead 12,000 men to attack David and his people immediately. "David and his people must be totally exhausted after fleeing you for almost a week, and their spirits have to be very low." Ahithophel emphasizes they must attack David's army before they reach the Jordan River. He assures Absalom when he has killed David all the people shall run to Absalom for protection. *And, the saying pleased Absalom and all the elders of Israel". (2 Samuel 17:4 NKJV)*

Before Ahithophel is given consent to proceed, Absalom sends for Hushai. Absalom shares Ahithophel's suggested strategy. He asks Hushai's opinion and Hushai instantly discounts Ahithophel's plan. As ordered, he begins influencing Absalom's thinking, "Your Highness, the army is angry, they conceive your actions as treason to King David's crown, and they are fuming because you displaced them and their families from their homes." Hushai reminds Absalom, "Those men, Ahithophel casually refers to, are a part of David's highly experienced army, led by Joab." (The risks of going to war, against David's army, are beginning to resonate with Absalom.) Hushai recommends, "Absalom, you should be more prudent and wait until you can build your own mighty army. A well-trained army is the only realistic way you can expect to defeat your father, and it is imperative you are triumphant at the first engagement. Accomplish that victory and you will be celebrated as the new warrior King." Ahithophel is furious, he is very familiar with this tactic; many times the King has given him the same assignment.

With his advice accepted, Hushai informs Zadok and Abiathar the results of his meeting: "Absalom is not taking Ahithophel's advice; but as a precaution, David should immediately get to the other side of the Jordan." The two sons, Jonathan and Ahimaaz, immediately depart to inform the King. They survive the dangers traveling through enemy lines only because villagers hid them along the way putting their own lives at risk; the people still had love for King David. The messengers arrive at dusk, whereupon David and the army waste no time assembling the people to rapidly get them across the river. The last group crosses over as the sun is rising. As they land on shore people from several villages are welcoming them with food, dry clothing, and other comforts. It is an indication of the villagers' joy to see their King, as well as their confidence that he will remain their King. God heard David's prayer *"For the LORD had purposed to defeat the good advice of Ahithophel, to the intent that the LORD might bring disaster on Absalom." (2 Samuel 17:14 NKJV)* The account demonstrates even while David is being chastised by God, God's instruments of punishment are only allowed to go so far; just as with us!

Ahithophel's was suspicious of Hushai's motives from the time of his appearance. His suspicions were justified; he knows he gave Absalom the best advice. Because of Ahithophel's keen knowledge of David's combat capabilities, he correctly understood a surprise attack on David was Absalom's only chance of defeating David. In his judgment Absalom could not overthrow David playing the long game. Ahithophel now realizes he chose the wrong side. His thirst for personal revenge interfered with this brilliant man's decision-making. Ahithophel went home, *"Then he put his household in order, and hanged himself, and died."* *(2 Samuel 17:23 NKJV)* One household matter Ahithophel put in order was solidifying Nathan's vow to care for his granddaughter and great grandson.

The Scripture gives no mention of David going to God before planning his battle against Absalom. Surely he was continuously praying and meditating during that long walk to the Jordan River. He would have spoken to God about his many apprehensions, particularly the regrettable, inevitable, encounter with his son. *"Then David sent out one third of the people under the hand of Joab, one third under the hand of Abishai the son of Zeruiah, Joab's brother, and one third under the hand of Ittai the Gittite."* *(2 Samuel 18:2 NKJV)* David publically gives a command to the three Generals "Be gentle with my son for my sake."

David's well trained army slaughters Absalom's "people's army." Absalom observes the massacre and flees riding a mule. Looking back to see if he has escaped, he rides under a low hanging branch of a terebinth tree, and his long flowing hair gets entangled in the branch. The mule continues running leaving Absalom hanging in the air. Joab's men witness the event and are bewildered; they rush to Joab and report. Joab vehemently questions why they didn't kill Absalom. Joab locates Absalom, *"And ten young men who bore Joab's armor surrounded Absalom, and struck and killed him."* *(2 Samuel 18:15 NKJV)*

Even though he is mindful of the King's personal request, "Be gentle with my son for my sake;" Joab ensures Absalom does not live. Joab believes David will eventually forgive Absalom and Absalom will sooner or later revolt again. Joab does not let emotion influence his decision to kill Absalom; it's just business. Joab asserts to his men he made the decision for the safety of the

King and the preservation of the Kingdom. The truth is Joab and Abishai had already concluded that Absalom was not the leader they would follow; Absalom became expendable.

Joab sends two messengers to inform the king of the battle's results. Zadok's son gets there first and tells David the good news, *"Blessed be Jehovah thy God, who hath delivered up the men that lifted up their hand against my lord the king." (2 Samuel 18:28 ASV)* David instantly asks about Absalom. Ahimaaz feels a chill go through his body; he recalls the stories of others who have brought the King bad news and recoils from answering. Fortunately for him, Joab's Cushite messenger arrives. David directs his attention to the Cushite servant and asks the welfare of his son. When David hears the answer he walks away grief-stricken. The victory's consequences brought sadness not only to David but, *"The victory that day was turned into mourning unto all the people; for the people heard say that day, The king grieveth for his son." (2 Samuel 19:2 ASV)*

After days of nationwide mourning, Joab admonishes David for making the people feel that he cares more about his enemies than those who risked their lives to save him and his family. Joab is pleased for this opportunity to display David's faults. Joab is one of the few who can speak to David in this manner; their time and nefarious deeds go way back. Joab advises David to get up and go comfort his servants or they will abandon him. Joab looks upon his reprimanding David as an opportunity for others to realize his status and recognize his capacity for leadership. *"Then the king arose, and sat in the gate. And they told unto all the people, saying, Behold, the king is sitting in the gate: and all the people came before the king." (2 Samuel 19:8 ASV)* David acknowledges that Joab's advice was prudent, but he also feels betrayed by Joab for letting Absalom get killed. Right now David is suppressing his anger, but it is brewing, even without yet knowing the truth of Absalom's death.

# CHAPTER 14

# REUNITING THE KINGDOM

"THEN SAID THE KING TO AMASA, ASSEMBLE ME
THE MEN OF JUDAH WITHIN THREE DAYS, AND BE
THOU HERE PRESENT."

2 SAMUEL 20:4 (KJV)

D avid is anxious to return to The City of David.  He has heard those leaders, who were once aligned with Absalom, are longing for the King's return.  David's resilience convinces the Elders they need him as their King, *"so that they sent unto the king, saying, Return thou, and all thy servants." (2 Samuel 19:14 ASV)* David sends Zadok and Abiathar to the City to discuss terms for reconciliation and David being their King again.  It is a joyous moment preparing to return back to the City.  It's a stark contrast to the emotions felt when they recently fled across the Jordan; now is a time for reunion and celebration.  The men of Judah, Shimei the stone thrower, and a thousand men of Benjamin, as well as Ziba from the house of Saul, act as a delegation to help with the Jordan crossing and the travel back home, *"And there went over a ferry-boat to bring over the king's household, and to do what he thought good." (2 Samuel 19:18 ASV)*

Shimei humbles himself to David asking for forgiveness for throwing rocks at the King during his escape from Absalom, and he asks not be put to death, *"But Abishai the son of Zeruiah answered and said, Shall not Shimei be put to death for this, because he cursed Jehovah's anointed?" (2 Samuel 19:21 ASV)* Abishai is expecting David to be consistent with his policy of giving respect to anointed individuals, but in this case David delays any action. David does not want to dampen the unification's festive mood; he publically forgives Shimei.

Mephibosheth shows up ragged, unshaven, and noticeably he hasn't bathed in a while. David inquires, "Mephibosheth, why did you not escape from The City along with the rest of us?" Mephibosheth mumbles several excuses, none that convince David. David tells him the land will be equally divided between him and Ziba. Mephibosheth pretends to be undeserving, he expresses unworthiness of any consideration; he suggests Ziba take all the land. At this time David doesn't care about the land's ownership; the politician in David is mending fences and promoting harmony. Shimei, Mephibosheth, and Ziba are Benjaminites and right now he needs Saul's countrymen to be on his side.

Continuing harmony-building gestures, David appoints Amasa, who was previously Absalom's Army General, to be the General of Israel's army. David is trying to demonstrate he wants to unite Israel, and that he does not intend to be a vengeful King. Amasa's appointment also acts as an explicit message to his nephews, "I am still in charge, I'm the King, and you serve at my pleasure." David's anger about Absalom's death is increasing. As gossip abounds, he is increasingly doubtful he's been told the truth about his son's death. David enjoyed knowing Joab was furious after he heard he had given Amasa his position!

Struggles to determine who will be closest to power are historical and common today; these power struggles tear countries apart. David has yet settled in The City and the political factions are already positioning themselves. The Israelites who fled the City with David are angry over all the preferential treatment their countrymen who supported Absalom are getting. Their position is, "Our once neighbors, who didn't leave with us, stayed and supported the coup; they deserve punishment not benefits. Our loyalty and sacrifices to the King should reap us the benefits." This split in the kingdom affords Sheba, another Benjaminite, the opportunity to arouse the Israelites who feel jilted, *"We have no portion in David, neither have we inheritance in the son of Jesse." (2 Samuel 20:1 ASV) "So all the men of Israel went up from following David, and followed Sheba the son of Bichri." (2 Samuel 20:2 ASV)* General Amasa's first assignment is to quickly find and eliminate Sheba.

After David regains the throne he quarantines his concubine; the ten women who were violated by Absalom. David assigns them to a secluded section of the palace. He provides for them but he never visits; they are widows, outcasts, victims again. He begins purging the villages of the persons who supported Absalom. Any expressions of animosity or envy towards David are squelched. Even the heirs of Absalom, David's grandsons, are tortured and terminated. Next David intends to meet with the leaders of Judah to make sure they understand who is in charge and that he is their King. He orders Amasa: *"Assemble me the men of Judah within three days, and be thou here present." (2 Samuel 20:4 KJV)*

The allotted time Amasa is given to bring the men of Judah and David together has long expired. Additionally, David is frustrated with Amasa's inability to capture Sheba. David's disappointment in Amasa forces him to recognize, and reluctantly acknowledge, he misses Joab. David contacts Abishai and complains how Sheba's uprising is promoting divisions in the country, and he must be stopped. And more to Abishai and Joab's interest, he rages about Amasa's incompetence in assembling the men of Judah, and especially in capturing Sheba. David orders Abishai to find Sheba. Abishai at once goes to Joab. He shares the King's negative comments about Amasa, and tells of his assignment to find Sheba.

Joab and Abishai have been searching two days for Sheba and while passing through Gibeon they run across none other than Amasa. Under the pretense of being pleased to see Amasa, Joab grabs his beard as a sign of brotherhood then thrust his sword into Amasa's stomach.

After witnessing Amasa's execution his men are given an ultimatum, *"And one of Joab's men stood by him, and said, He that favoureth Joab, and he that is for David, let him go after Joab." (2 Samuel 20:11 KJV)* Amasa's men join Joab and the united armies proceed to locate Sheba the son of Bichri; they find him hiding in Abel-Beth Maachah. As the army is readying to attack, a wise woman calls out from behind the city walls requesting to speak to Joab. She comes out the gate, meets Joab, and begins to barter, "Will you spare the city and its occupants if I can persuade the people to turn Sheba over to you?" Before responding, Joab threatens, "Sheba raised his hand against the King so he must die, and who ever gives Sheba safe harbor shall die as well." Joab agrees not to attack if the people produce Sheba, and he assures her he does not want to destroy their city. She declares, *"Watch, his head will be throne to you over the wall." (2 Samuel 20:21 NKJV)* Joab returns to the City of David after eliminating Amasa, and with Sheba's head in hand.

So whose objectives are realized? David hated Amasa for those grueling days he led Absalom's army that chased the King and his people out of the City. David vividly remembers hundreds of frightened women and children, the sick and elderly, hastily walking over 140 torturous miles. He curses Amasa for the inerasable pictures in his mind of the people struggling, with their children, belongings, and livestock, crossing the Jordan River's 6 feet of flowing water.

Publically announcing the promotion of Amasa as the new Commander of Israel's Army was David's first covert step to repay Amasa; he knew Joab would be furious and react. When David commanded Abishai to find Sheba, he knew Abishai would go to Joab, and he anticipated they would likely encounter Amasa while searching for Sheba. David had no doubt if they met Joab would kill Him. Equally pleasing to David, Joab will be blamed for Amasa's death; the theme of their long relationship. Aware of Joab's disregard for his authority and his trust for him diminished, David is still mindful that at this time Joab has unrivaled value.

For Joab, he feels he's getting closer to reaching his objectives. He has repeatedly proven to the King and demonstrated to the people he is the true leader of the army; the same army King David and the people rely on to exist as a free people. Joab is vindicated when David publically acknowledges Joab's status by reappointing him as Commander. *"And Joab was over all the army of Israel." (2 Samuel 20:23 NKJV)*

After two decades Joab is increasingly envious and still mystified why God provides repeated gifts and favors to David. Joab's mystification of David, similar to David's brothers' ignorance and envy of him, derives from none of them paying attention to David's Spiritual life. They had no awareness of how much effort David put into building his intimate relationship with Jehovah. They cannot connect David's devotion to God as the reason he's favored. Joab concludes God's favor to David is now at an end. Consequently, he now considers them both equals and both Godless. Joab may yearn for God's massive power and His benefits to be on his side; but he doesn't long for God's love, or His relationship. Joab believes he is self-sufficient. Dr. Charles Stanley, Pastor of First Baptist Church, Atlanta, GA says, "No one gets what he really wants by supplying his own needs."[10]

# CHAPTER 15

# GOD'S DISPLEASURE

"AND AGAIN THE ANGER OF THE LORD WAS KINDLED
AGAINST ISRAEL, AND HE MOVED DAVID AGAINST
THEM TO SAY, GO, NUMBER ISRAEL AND JUDAH."
(2 SAMUEL 24:12)

A famine persists in Israel for three years. David sees this as a continuation of his punishment for sins. He inquires of the Lord through an Oracle, "Why is there a drought?" He's told Saul's killing of the Gibeonites violated the treaty made with Joshua. The treaty specified the two nations will live beside each other peacefully, and the Israelites are responsible for their protection. *"Wherefore David said unto the Gibeonites, What shall I do for you? and wherewith shall I make the atonement that ye may bless the inheritance of the LORD?" (2 Samuel 21:3 KJV)* The Gibeonites don't want gold or silver, nothing material; they want death to Saul's family members. David and the Gibeonites see eye to eye; David selects seven from Saul's family, *"And he delivered them into the hands of the Gibeonites, and they hanged them in the hill before the LORD." (2 Samuel 21:9 KJV)* After the burial of the seven and the bones of Saul and Jonathan are buried in the tomb of Saul's father, Kish, the rain arrives revitalizing the crops. The selection of the seven sacrificed family members means David does not honor Saul's request for mercy on his family. But since Mephibosheth was deliberately not a candidate in the selection process, David ensured he would keep his pledge to Jonathon.

Troubles persist: *"Satan stood up against Israel, and moved David to number Israel." (1 Chronicles 21:1 NKJV).* Some ask why God would allow Satan *"to move David* to sin." God *"moves"* whomever he pleases, by whomever He chooses, to accomplish His purpose. The real questions are, how will David respond to Satan's challenge, and to whose voice is he listening? In the past David always reached out to God at the first appearance of a military challenge. David would then be assured of success regardless of how many men he or his enemy had. But in the past David was also a humble individual, who thanked God for what He had done and continuously looked to God for direction and protection. Since becoming King, David has been selective with his petitions to God as is the case now. David counting the people to determine his ability to win a battle, and not asking for God's support and blessings, is an affront to God.

David summons Joab to conduct a census. Joab first questions the command sighting political reasons, "I don't want to enrage the people who will have concerns about another bloody war, and second, the captains will grumble about getting deployed so soon, and leaving their families." Joab's worries did not deter David. Joab then sarcastically asks David, "Why does a pious person like yourself need to measure your military capability; why aren't you going to God for your answers?" Joab challenges David with the same Spiritual wisdom he's heard David espouse repeatedly. Joab's question is two-fold, to stave off the drudgery of executing a census, and to assess the current status of David and God's relationship. David ignores Joab's mockery, and evidently he has no intention of reaching out to God. *"Notwithstanding the king's word prevailed against Joab, and against the captains of the host."* *(2 Samuel 24:4 KJV)* Joab gathers his men and proceeds to travel across the nation for almost ten months tallying the number of men available to fight for the King; over a million able bodied men are identified. Joab obediently, though reluctantly, fulfills his assigned mission.

After reading Joab's report David experiences many restless nights. He is startled one morning, and awakes in a cold sweat. He is deeply remorseful for ordering the counting of the people. David becomes conscious to the fact that his gathering a census was an act of pride. The realization that he is falling further out of God's will and deeper into Satan's clutches frightens him. He is becoming aware of the seductive attributes the crown cultivates within a person: pride, privilege, prestige, and a thirst for power. Pride and prestige are two vulnerable characteristics Satan detects in David, and he has been taking advantage of both.

David begins praying and confesses he has sinned. At that moment, Gad the Prophet is knocking on his door with a message from God, *"Thus saith the LORD, I offer thee three things; choose thee one of them, that I may do it unto thee;"* *(2 Samuel 24:12 KJV)* Of the three options, *"David said to Gad let me not fall into the hand of man."* *(2 Samuel 24:14 KJV)* David chooses a plague on the people. As a result of his decision, 70,000 Israelites die from the plague before David regrets his choice and implores the Lord, *"Let thine hand, I pray thee, be against me, and against my father's house."* *(2 Samuel 24:17 KJV)*

An angel commands Gad, "Inform David he must build the Lord an altar on a nearby threshing floor." Araunah the Jebusite, hears of God's command to David and without hesitation, offers to donate the threshing floor along with the oxen, for the Lord's altar and sacrifice. David, knowing the purchase price is a part of his penance explains to Araunah he could not sacrifice to God *"that which cost me nothing"*. David respectfully declines and pays Araunah *"the full price"* of six hundred shekels of gold. *"And David built there an altar to the LORD, and offered burnt offerings and peace offerings. So the LORD heeded the prayers for the land, and the plague was withdrawn from Israel."* (2 Samuel 24:25 NKJV) This location where God chose to build the altar is the location where Solomon eventually builds the Temple to house the Ark of the Covenant.

Gad chides David, "God has always had a plan for you, stop getting in the way. You are being shown the error of your ways, and experiencing the cost of disobedience. You should realize by now God has selected you to bring His people into a closer relationship with their Heavenly Father. You can't complete your mission with the gap you've created between you and our Lord. David, your people's hopes and dreams for Israel are joined to you; the realizations of their dreams are contingent upon your transparent obedience and faithfulness to God. If you sincerely continue to repent, as you have humbly expressed in your Psalms, you will be able to move ever closer to God enabling you to faithfully fulfill your assignment."

# CHAPTER 16

# THE FAMILY CULTURE

AND HE CONFERRED WITH JOAB THE SON OF
ZERUIAH, AND WITH ABIATHAR THE PRIEST: AND
THEY FOLLOWING ADONIJAH HELPED HIM.

1KINGS 1:7 (KJV)

Another swipe by God's sword is Adonijah's obsession and his strategy to take possession of the throne.  Presently, Adonijah is the oldest living heir to the throne since both older brothers, Amnon and Absalom, have been killed.  Adonijah believes Absalom allowed his resentment towards their father to influence his judgment.  Absalom was seen by most as an angry revengeful son eager to punish his father.  He tried to portray himself as a person who, if King, would greatly improve the masses lives.  But the people were aware of why Absalom wanted to dislodge King David from the throne; not the deception he perpetrated to them for 4 years.  And when Absalom publically revealed the names of his leadership team it confirmed the certainty of who he really was and his motives.

In spite of Absalom's failed coup, Adonijah is optimistic and encouraged he will succeed.  He and his brother share many of the same negative feelings towards their father but Adonijah's strategy is more insightful, and his motive appears positive and rationale. He enlightens the people of the King's failing health that previously has been kept secret. Adonijah has been closely monitoring his father's declining health, and he notifies the people, "Your King is unable to stand unassisted or even sit for long periods of time, and more often than not, he is lying in bed." Adonijah emphasizes the urgency for a smooth transition of the crown to ensure the continued security and prosperity of the Kingdom.

Adonijah is further convinced of his argument's merits when he hears of the healing treatment prescribed for the comatose King. *"Now King David was old, advanced in years; and they put covers on him, but he could not get warm. Therefore his servants said to him, "Let a young woman, a virgin, be sought for our lord the king, and let her stand before the king, and let her care for him; and let her lie in your bosom, that our lord the king may be warm."* (1 Kings 1:1-2 NKJV).

During these times it is believed that the warmth of a body may help revive a dying person whose body does not self-produce heat, and therefore the prescription. Some biographers believe the prescription was written because of the servants' credible fear of caring for David. The servants agree with the prescribed treatment; they know the King is very ill, or possibly dying, and he is not responding. But none of them are willing to risk their life by startling David, either by putting their hand on him, examining him, or shaking him. What will the King's response be to the person who wakes him?

The servants also believe the prescription is a good choice based on another known characteristic of David: *the lust in his heart.* *"A young woman, a virgin, be sought for our lord the king."* *"So they sought for a lovely young woman throughout all the territory of Israel, and found Abishag the Shunammite, and brought her to the king." (1 Kings 1:3 NKJV).* Russell Dilday says, in his book, *Mastering the Old Testament, 1, 2 Kings,* "Obviously, Abishag was to be more than a nurse to the king." The Septuagint translation makes it specific: "Let her excite him and lie with him".[11] *"The young woman was very lovely; and she cared for the king, and served him; but the king did not know her." (1 Kings 1:4 NKJV).* Adonijah learns about his father's lack of virility, which in his and most other's minds, is positive evidence of the King's declining health. The news of the King's failure to get *"excited"* pleases Adonijah even more for a personal reason, he has his eye on the lovely Abishag the Shunammite; Adonijah covets her for himself.

With this new revelation of the King's poor health, Adonijah feels this is an opportune time to lay claim to the throne. Staying in the public eye, he pays tribute to himself by mimicking Absalom and has 50 men run before his horse drawn chariot as a sign of his royalty. More important, Adonijah chooses a competent leadership team compared to his brother. *"Then he conferred with Joab the son of Zeruiah and with Abiathar the priest, and they followed and helped Adonijah." (1 Kings 1:7 NKJV).* Joab and Abishai, have been seeking the right opportunity to leave David and Adonijah seems their best chance. Abiather is the last priest of the house of Eli. He feels David only keeps him around to assuage his guilt feelings regarding the deaths of those at the City of Nob. Abiather concluded long ago David favored Zadok over him and so he opted for this opportunity to be the Spiritual leader.

Nathan, who has been suspicious of Adonijah's royal ambitions for some time, receives a report from his network of priests concerning Adonijah's proposed coronation. Nathan is deeply aware of who God expects to be the next person on the throne.

Nathan witnessed God's pleasure at the birth of Solomon, calling him, *"Jedidiah, beloved of God."* Nathan painfully remembers another piece of evidence; God admonishing him for encouraging David to build a temple for the Ark of the Covenant, when God had planned for Solomon to have that honor. Nathan feels God intricately involved him with the David and Bathsheba drama, *"for such a time as this";* to ensure God's will for Solomon materializes.

Nathan quickly reacts to the news of the coronation. He rushes to Bathsheba, explains what's happening, and gives her warning, "If Adonijah becomes King, with his accomplice Joab, you and Solomon's lives are in peril." Bathsheba was not aware of this plot, but she doesn't doubt it, nor is she surprised. Bathsheba has always known David's older sons detested Solomon, and the plot confirmed David's long-term belief of Joab's deceitfulness and disloyalty. Nathan and Bathsheba were confident David was not cognizant of the latest coup attempt. Unknown to most, the King these days is quite aloof regarding daily affairs.

Nathan takes charge and orchestrates a plan, *"Go immediately to King David and say to him, 'Did you not, my lord, O king, swear to your maidservant, saying, "Assuredly your son Solomon shall reign after me, and he shall sit on my throne?" Why then has Adonijah become king?" (1 Kings 1:13 NKJV).* Nathan assures Bathsheba, "As you are petitioning the King I will enter the room and corroborate your information and support your appeal."

Bathsheba meets with the King and as she finishes her prepared script, Nathan arrives. David excuses Bathsheba so he and Nathan can speak privately. Nathan confirms Bathsheba's petition, and he emphasizes, "Joab and Abishai have joined Adonijah and they are traitors to you, my King." Nathan reminds David of God's words, *"He will build a house for My name, and I will establish the throne of his kingdom forever." (2 Samuel 7:13 NKJV)* The "he" in God's message is Solomon, and everyone including David, all his family, and associates, know who God predestined to be the next King. The latter people observed David for years make meticulous preparations for the Temple's construction to be managed by David and Bathsheba's prophesized son.

The attempt to prevent Solomon from fulfilling God's wishes alarms and infuriates David. It lights a fire in him; he becomes lucid, makes critical decisions, and gives directives. He calls Bathsheba back in the room and gives her his oath that Solomon will be the next King. He instructs his three loyalists, Zadok, Nathan, and Benaiah to ride Solomon through the streets on his mule, along with his personal bodyguards. David knows the symbolism will be seen as evidence of Solomon's accent to the throne. He instructs the trustworthy three to take Solomon to the sanctuary tent in Gihon where the Ark of the Covenant is kept. *"There let Zadok the priest and Nathan the prophet anoint him king over Israel; and blow the horn, and say, 'Long live King Solomon!" (1 Kings 1:34 NKJV)* The people and the Elders were overjoyed to see the throne transferring smoothly from David to Solomon. They reach out to David praising him for his selection; they ask God to make Solomon a caring ruler like his father. Lying in his bed, David bows himself and thanks the Lord for letting him live to see Solomon sit on the throne.

Adonijah is hosting his crowning ceremony. He has invited his brothers and all the dignitaries with exceptions, *"But he did not invite Nathan the prophet, Benaiah, the mighty men, or Solomon his brother." (1 Kings 1:10 NKJV)* No mystery why he did not invite them, those named were all loyal to King David. No surprise Joab with his self-serving motives was there; his dwindling loyalty to David has been noticed for years and he is finally showing his true colors. While attending the celebration Joab sees a rider at

a distance approaching rapidly.  It is Abiather's son, Jonathan, arriving from the City.  Breathing heavily, he informs Joab that King
David has made Solomon King.  He reports how Zadok and Nathan
anointed Solomon and, *"Also Solomon sits on the throne of the
kingdom." (1 Kings 1:46 NKJV)*

Overhearing the news of Solomon being made King; all of
Adonijah's supporters scatter.  Adonijah fears what Solomon will
do to him so he takes off to the sanctuary thinking he'll be safe by
taking hold of the *"horns of the altar."* Russell Dilday in his book
*Mastering the Old Testament* describes the horns of the altar and
its tradition: "The horns were wooden projections overlaid with
brass protruding from the four corners of the altar.  The practice
of finding safety in the sanctuary was common enough among the
various cultures in the Near East.  It should be noted though; this
act of asylum was intended to protect innocent people."[12]

Solomon hears of Adonijah's plea for mercy and momentarily
grants him a conditional reprieve; Adonijah must *"prove himself
a worthy person."* This is an occasion when Solomon's wisdom is
on display.  His first command as King, forgiving Andonijah, is perceived as an example of his capacity for mercy.  For now Solomon
is not concerned about getting justice or revenge.  He knows when
the time comes for their confessions Adonijah and his cohorts will
not be able to defend themselves for their treasonous acts.

# CHAPTER 17

# LEAVE NO LOOSE ENDS

FOR WE ARE STRANGERS BEFORE THEE, AND
SOJOURNERS, AS WERE ALL OUR FATHERS: OUR
DAYS ON THE EARTH ARE AS A SHADOW, AND THERE
IS NONE ABIDING."

1 CHRONICLES 29:15

K ing David calls a conference with the Princes and leaders of the people. *"King David said to all the assembly: "My son Solomon, whom alone God has chosen, is young and inexperienced." (1 Chronicles 29:1 NKJV)* David wants all the leaders to hear from his mouth who is the next King. While on his deathbed David passes the scepter to Solomon. With Solomon's lack of experience in mind, David gives him some final advice: "Keep God's laws and you will *prosper in all that you do and wherever you turn.* Put to death your cousin Joab because of the unwarranted killings he has committed (David knows Joab's cunning and ambition will be too much for Solomon to manage at his young age). Show gratitude to Barzillia because during Absalom's rebellion he supported me throughout my flight from the City. And, execute Shemei for cursing and throwing stones at me during that same period."

David and Solomon being Co-Regents of Israel comes to an end. *"So David rested with his fathers, and was buried in the City of David." (1 Kings 2:10 NKJV).* Solomon is now the King of Israel with Bathsheba as the Queen Mother. Early in Solomon's reign he fulfills his father's last wishes by killing Joab, Shemei, and many other adversaries, be they family members or not. He rewards Nathan by making him the nation's Spiritual leader and places his sons in government positions. Solomon is *a chip off the old block.*

# EPILOGUE

Jonathan Kirsch, a Member of the National Book Critics Circle says, "Above all, David illustrates the fundamental truth that the sacred and the profane may find full expression in a single human life, and his biography preserves the earliest evidence of the neurotic double bind that is hardwired into human nature and tugs each one of us in different directions at once. Against every effort of Bible-waving moralizers who seek to make us better than we are— or to make us feel bad about the way we are –the Biblical account of David is there to acknowledge and even to affirm what men and women really feel and really do."[13]

An often asked question, "How can we compare our lives to those in the Old Testament; it's so long ago and things were so different?" We are able to compare our life experiences as believers, to their lives as believers, because our histories are linked to the same God. Throughout history men and women have tried to be obedient in their time and place. We are trying to do the same. All of us, then and now, are God's children trying to live in this same sinful world while endeavoring to be compliant to His doctrine. David and his people worshiped the same God we worship today; He has not changed. Our unchanging God binds us together. What He wanted from believers then, God wants from His children now; for us to be loving and obedient.

The credentialed Bible Scholar, Donald Harman Akenson speaking of David In the book, *The Real Life of the Man Who Ruled Israel* says, "He is the first full-formed figure to be found in the

Bible, and, indeed, is probably the first human being for whom we have a biography."[14] David's story reveals to us how God will support and provide when we are, *and often when we are not*, in His will. He'll guide our path, fight our battles, and comfort us, as only He can, with His peace. God will also reprimand us when we get off our assigned path, and continuously coax us to get back on it; as He did with David then, and He does with us now. Graciously God's arms were always open to welcome and forgive a repentant David, and when we repent, His arms are still wide open. We must keep in mind, as David discovered, God's forgiveness does not mean a price will not be paid for the sin. But during the period of reprimand it was comforting for David to know God was present. God has not changed His behavior; He is with us during our periods of chastisement. God continues *"To be a lamp unto our feet and a light to our pathway."*

Notice David's tendency to drift away from God after he had accomplished the inexplicable, and prospered beyond all expectations. Beware of the accolades you hear for your achievements. Always acknowledge to yourself and others the reason why those complements are being given. Forget not what caused those achievements to materialize. Continue the behavior that brought you to where you have arrived; but do not fail to remember Who got you there.

Be on notice, if you drift away, expect God to always do His part to bring you back to Him; He's relentless. We may not enjoy His corrective teachings, but be comforted knowing He's there with you. And don't forget, in the midst of the storm it is imperative to stay focused on our Almighty God, for waiting to be gleaned amid the turmoil is His wisdom.

We all are human, and everyone has his or her own road to travel; a path we tend to encumber with our predilection to be worldly.  Just like David, unexpected troubles will arise in our lives; therefore, it is critical who we reflexively choose to be with us during those storms! We can be grateful, for we are more fortunate than those in David's time.  We have Jesus Christ, our Lord and Savior to call on, and we have been given 66 Books in the Bible that illustrate how to walk with, and be obedient to God.  Take advantage of both gifts, stay in His Word.  And, *"Do not be anxious about anything, but in every situation, by prayer and petition, with thanksgiving, present your requests to God." (Philippians 4:6 KJV*)

Prayerfully, reading this book has shined some light on David's life and at the same time lets you better see the **LIGHT** shining in yours! And always keep in mind; you are God's beloved too!!!

# NOTES

M-1 The Bible Journey [pg-V]

#1 Men of Character, David, Seeking God Faithfully Dr. Gene A. Geltz, Page 1 [pg-VII]

#2 Mastering the Old Testament, 1, 2 Samuel; Kenneth Chafin; Page 300 [pg-VIII]

#3 David's Secret Demons, Baruch Halperns; Pages 10-12 [pg-15]

#4 Bible History Old Testament, 1 Samuel 22; [pg-21]

#5 Jonathan Kirsch, author of "King David (The Real Life of The Man Who Ruled Israel)" [pg-33]

#6 The Sins of King David Gary Greenberg, page 1 [pg-43]

#7 Jamieson-Fausset-Brown Bible Commentary; 2 Samuel 7:12 [pg-50]

#8 Jamieson-Fausset-Brown Bible Commentary; 2 Samuel 7:12 [pg-51]

#9 "He is called in 1 Chronicles 27:33 "the king's friend." This title is similar to that of counselor given to Ahithophel, or that of leader of the army to Joab; it is an official title given by the Seleucids to persons of confidence who have important military or civil functions; Wikipedia: Hushai; [pgs-71]

#10 In-Touch Daily Reader, Dr. Charles Stanley, July 8, 2017, Page 13, [pg-84]

#11 Mastering the Old Testament, 1, 2 Kings; Russell Dilday; Page 30; [pg-91]

#12 Mastering the Old Testament, 1, 2 Kings; Russell Dilday; Page 47; [94]

#13 King David, The Real Life of The Man Who Ruled Israel; Jonathan Kirsch; Chapter One, Page 2 [pg-97]

#14 King David, The Real Life of The Man Who Ruled Israel: a Donald Harman Akenson quote, Page 295 [pg-97

www.ingramcontent.com/pod-product-compliance
Lightning Source LLC
Chambersburg PA
CBHW030236180626
46810CB00008B/3161